GRAVE WATERS

Two cunning, cold-blooded killers board the cruise ship *Nerissa* disguised as an elderly couple, with a deadly armoury at their disposal courtesy of the Russian Mafia. Meanwhile, members of a mysterious cult called the Foundation have infiltrated the passenger list, with their own sinister agenda to take over the ship. When they strike, they disrupt the on-board wedding ceremony of police officer David Spaulding. Can the ship's captain, aided by David and his new friend, author and anthropologist Richard Black Wolf, regain control of the *Nerissa* before it's too late?

ANA R. MORLAN
AND MARY W. BURGESS

GRAVE
WATERS

Complete and Unabridged

LINFORD
Leicester

First published in Great Britain

First Linford Edition
published 2016

A catalogue record for this book is available
from the British Library.

ISBN 978–1–4448–2773–6

1

Mildred O'Conner took her third sip of champagne in as many miles as they'd been on the road. *That girlie from the cruise line is putting a move on my Norman,* she told herself.

The uniformed young couple from the Contessa Lines had arrived half an hour early at the O'Conners' home in Barrington Hills, Illinois. They parked their limo close to the front walk so neither of them would have to walk too far down the icy driveway.

The woman had flourished a bottle of bubbly and couldn't seem to keep her eyes off Norman. Well, Norman never minded attention, Mildred decided with a gentle chuckle as the champagne's bubbles tingled against her nose.

But this girlie seemed . . . different, somehow.

'So, Mr. O'Conner, the trustees of the bank elected *you* president over all those

1

other men? That must've been a real honor,' the girl said as she tucked him in with a robe, then hopped into the front with the driver.

Mildred snorted over Norman's reply.

'Was *indeed* an honor, Miss . . . now what did you say your name was, dearie?'

The young woman turned all the way around in her seat so that she was facing them. She smiled at Norman before answering in a slightly accented voice, 'Morgance Searlait.' ('*Seer-Lay*,' she pronounced it for him.) 'And I can imagine how proud *you* must've been, Mrs. O'Conner,' she added, turning to Mildred, 'when your husband was promoted.'

My husband got the damned promotion because he was the outgoing president's wife's cousin, Mildred thought, nodding in reply.

The driver suddenly muttered, 'Oh God, what was that I just hit?'

'Are you sure you hit something, Nevin?' Morgance asked. 'I felt nothing.' She turned back to the passengers. 'Did either of you feel anything? A bump?'

They shook their heads.

Morgance glanced out the side windows at a thick, dark cluster of trees to the east that made up a broad nature preserve. They were well past Barrington Hills now, and even though the woods were uniformly dark, the tops of the trees loomed jaggedly against the clear moonlit skies beyond.

After a moment she said, 'I thought I saw a deer running. Perhaps . . . ?'

Mildred felt queasy. *Maybe it's the bubbly*, she told herself.

'I'm sure I hit something — a squirrel or a dog,' Nevin insisted. 'I'd hate to have that hanging on the grill when we drive into O'Hare.'

'Perhaps you'd best go back and take a look. Whatever it is might be hurt.' Morgance's voice sounded just a bit forced.

Nevin pulled to a stop, carefully made a U-turn, and retraced their course for a hundred yards or so.

The cold blast of air that marked his exit from the car was a wake-up slap against Mildred's thickly rouged cheek, and for a second she found herself staring intently at the remains of the bubbly she'd poured into her glass, thinking, *The color, and the taste . . . it isn't quite right . . .*

Morgance leaned over the partition again. 'Have you two been on any of the Contessa ships before?'

'More times than I can count,' Norman replied as the driver's silhouette moved against the surrounding darkness beyond the car to the rear of the vehicle. Abruptly, he knelt and vanished down somewhere near the left rear wheel well.

Odd, Mildred thought. *Maybe he has hit something, after all.*

'No wonder they chose you for the Preferred Customer Award,' Morgance was saying. Her voice was a bit mechanical, as if she were reading lines from a play. In fact, it sounded just like the certified letter the O'Conners had received three weeks ago — the one telling them they'd won this trip to the Caribbean.

But that's not right! Mildred's head was beginning to ache. Didn't the letter say they'd been picked at random from all

4

other the cruise customers?

Mildred had the question on her lips when she felt a rocking motion under the limo. Norman noticed it too and glanced at her for a second, his watery eyes darting behind his glasses. He turned back to Morgance. 'What *was* that, missy?'

'I'm sure Nevin will tell us what happened,' Morgance said smoothly. 'Why don't you both have a little more champagne?'

Nevin opened and closed the car door very quickly this time, so that the frigid blast was intercepted by the steady push of warm air from the heater.

The car was moving smoothly down the highway again before he said, 'False alarm, folks. Didn't see so much as a whisker from any animal.'

The thought caused Mildred's stomach to lurch. She shouldn't have had so much champagne. Her vision was blurry and her head throbbed.

She was relieved when Nevin said, 'I think our guests might like a little privacy, *oui*?' before he pressed a button on the dashboard.

As the thick glass partition sealed the O'Conners completely off from the front part of the limo, Mildred decided that a little nap might do her some good and, as her head fell against Norman's shoulder, she noticed his eyes were drooping, too, now that the cruise-line girlie wasn't distracting him any longer.

Glancing at their charges, Nevin waited until he saw both of the old people close their eyes before reaching down to the floorboard for a small cylinder of oxygen. He noted with satisfaction that the passenger compartment was already hazy, as if good old Norman and Mildred were smoking cigars, instead of slumped against each other with their eager mouths open and their wrinkled eyelids shut fast.

Nevin motioned for Morgance to assist him in attaching his mask as he drove. She'd already slipped on hers, the gelid plastic resting like a glove over her nose. As she positioned his face-piece and snaked the elastic strap around his head, she whispered to him, her voice distorted by the opaque covering, 'How long will we have to keep driving?'

'Two hours minimum,' he said, 'if the exhaust is giving off enough fumes. We can crack our windows a bit in the final hour.'

Morgance fiddled with the crackling car radio until Nevin reached over and shut it off. He did not want to rouse their cargo. He sighed. Morgance was very high-maintenance, and could be a holy terror if she didn't get her way.

They had many more miles of driving on Illinois back roads before this first stage was completed and they could turn around and head back to Barrington Hills.

★   ★   ★

Rifle at the ready, veteran Pittsburgh police officer David Spaulding stepped into the suspect's house, his eyes straining in the semi-darkness. His heart was thudding wildly, pumping so hard it felt as if it might beat straight through his Kevlar-encased chest before bursting out of the dark blue uniform. With each cautious step he took, deeper and deeper into the unknown, his ears strained to decipher the static-garbled words coming through the small radio unit attached to his left shoulder.

You'll get him, you'll find him, he kept telling himself. *You'll be the one to stop this madman from doing any more harm*.

But as he rounded a corner in the narrow hallway, the crackling of the radio near his ear gave way to the increasing blare of a television set turned up to the highest possible volume.

No sign of the suspect, but he shouted the standard alert. 'Police! Put down your weapon, now!' he called out over the racket that assaulted his eardrums.

He sensed the all-too-familiar tang of body odor in his nostrils. The suspect had to be close by.

He yelled out the warning again. The din from the television mocked him.

Reflexively curling his finger against the trigger of his cocked weapon, Spaulding continued down the hallway, the soles of his shoes slipping on loose pages of old newspapers scattered about on the matted carpeting.

A spill of pale gold pooled on the floor before him. The patch of bright sunlight was marred by an approaching shadow — a moving dark blob whose upraised right arm culminated in the unmistakable silhouette of a long-barrel. It appeared parallel to the doorway opening, a length of shining metal glinting like a thin ribbon of light as the suspect entered the hallway, first a foot and leg, followed by the rest of him.

Spaulding simultaneously grunted and pulled the trigger, even as the man kept coming toward him, his wide frame filling the narrow hallway, blocking the policeman's path and the light beyond.

The sound of the rifle's blast was a palpable presence in the small, close space — even before the man's chest blossomed with spreading thick red petals.

Spaulding was punched backwards by the rifle's kick against his shoulder. He hit the wall and his feet slid out from under him on the yellowed pages of the *Pittsburgh Post-Gazette*.

Even as he hit the floor, the sound of the blast kept coming and coming, until he realized it was just the television roaring a few feet away from his victim's lifeless head. It was an old black-and-white set, its wood-grain surface worn from years of handling. But the sound was still painfully clear even if the image was poor, marred by thin lines of white between the rows of pixels.

It was hard to make out the body of the suspect, prone against the even darker carpet. But once Spaulding got back on his feet, he could see his own image outlined clearly against the flickering TV screen, like a glowing grotesque roach in that small, stifling, trash-strewn room.

Spaulding shouldered his rifle and ran for the front doorway. It was standing wide open, although strangely, no other officers had entered the house. And, as he gazed at a patch of cobalt twilight above the surrounding row houses and street beyond, he imagined dozens of rifles taking aim at him, their barrels suddenly gleaming bright as searing hot bullets peppered his arms, his face, his legs;

10

sinking deeper and deeper, hitting blood and bone, and bursting like silent fireworks into his flesh . . .

Raking the soaking bedclothes with his hands, fingers gripping crumpled wads of fabric, Spaulding felt his heart flop with a painful thud in his chest.

Beside him, Deborah turned towards him, the soft sag of her breasts touching his shoulder. She drew her hand along his jawline, the tender skin catching on his beard stubble with a whispering rasp. 'Same dream, Dave?'

He swallowed hard, nodding his head against the pillow, and gave her hand a squeeze.

After a moment, he got up and went to the window. Pushing aside the curtains, he gazed out at the cityscape — downtown Pittsburgh. Streetlights winked icy-bright against black-silhouetted bridges, skyscrapers and the stadium. Moonlight reflected on the black patches of still-running water in the Allegheny's free-flowing swirls of quicksilver. Across the river, he could just make out the university's nearest buildings.

Deborah's voice came from behind him. 'Was it the TV dream again? And then they're shooting at you when you step out the door?'

He nodded.

'Oh God,' she moaned. 'But it's going to be okay now,' she continued. 'Remember, they found you innocent of any wrongdoing. The grand jury was only out a couple of hours. Why can't *that* part be in your dream?'

'Nightmare,' he corrected her as he watched intermittent car headlights move over the bridges. Within a few more hours he and Deb would be on one of those bridges, too — on their way out of here.

'Nightmare, then,' she agreed. 'And it will all end tomorrow night, once we're on that cruise ship. We'll be far away from this nightmare then, right, babe?'

'But Carl's going — Chip, too. They were *there* that night, right outside that house.'

'And they were also at the hearing,' she interrupted him. 'They know you're innocent. Even if they . . . well, even if they have made stupid comments from

12

time to time. And come tomorrow, we'll be sailing off to a place where nobody's heard of Pittsburgh, or anything that ever happened here.' She paused, then: 'Did you look at that brochure from the *Nerissa*?'

David touched his forehead to the cool window glass. She was only trying to help. But she was as aware as he was of the ramifications of the federal consent decree he and all the other cops had been saddled with as a result of his screw-up. Not to mention the FBI investigation — the inevitable result of a cop killing a civilian under any circumstance.

Still, Deb was just trying to get their lives back in order — even if he was still suspended in a numbing emotional void . . .

'Yeah, Deb,' he finally lied. 'I looked at it.'

'They have *everything* on that ship,' she went on enthusiastically. 'Clothing stores, casinos, restaurants — not to mention the wedding chapel.'

David didn't answer. He continued to rest his head against the cold glass and tried to think of nothing . . . nothing at all . . .

★ ★ ★

Nevin parked the limo as close to the front porch as he could without scratching the side of the car against the jutting stone finials of the portico. Even so, dragging the unconscious O'Conners into their house was a difficult task. Morgance hooked her arms around Norman's upper body and sidled backwards up the stone steps. His head bumped against her abdomen with each upward hoist, and she was rather surprised that the frail old man was so damned heavy.

Nevin, ahead of her, hitched his hands under Mildred's armpits, just over the saggy breasts. With each upward step he made, the old woman's wrinkled jaw thumped down hard on his crossed wrists.

'Careful,' Morgance hissed. 'You don't want to knock out her dentures, and I don't want to have to look for them.'

Nevin grunted and slid the body smoothly the rest of the way up the stairs up to the front door before asking, '*Qui avait les clefs — le quel ou la quelle?* Which one has the keys?'

'I don't know. Let me look.' She wished that they'd left the porch light on.

'Check his pockets first.' Nevin leaned against the wall and took a deep breath.

Morgance let the old man slide down along her leg to plop heavily on her feet as she lightly patted down his pockets, feeling a slight twinge of bile shoot up her throat as she detected his residual body warmth through her ungloved fingers.

There — in the right pocket. Propping open the storm door with her body, she tried the keys one by one in the lock.

'We're in.'

Nevin dragged Mildred in and dropped her on the tiled foyer floor, then turned to help Morgance drag Norman in before locking the front door behind them.

He wasn't particularly worried they would be seen; the O'Conners' house was on the outskirts of a small town. The next house stood empty and dark, and the property across the street bore a forlorn 'For Sale by Owner' sign in the front yard. Still, time was of the essence.

Just beyond the entry, dark wood paneling stood out in stark contrast to burnt-orange shag carpeting. Furnishings upholstered in avocado green and gold completed the dated '70s décor.

Nevin and Morgance conferred urgently. 'They'd look pretty good in these chairs, eh?' said the former.

'Well, help get his jacket off then.'

'Shall we take their shoes off? *Non? Oui?*'

'How about the TV — on or off?'

Once they'd stripped off the O'Conners' jackets and half-lifted, half-threw them onto their matching recliners, Nevin paused, then said, '*Où crois-tu que la porte du sous-sol se trouve?*'

'The door to the basement? It's probably out there,' she answered, pointing down the hall.

The two parted wordlessly. Nevin hurried out to the car and Morgance entered the kitchen, where she quickly spotted the passage that had to lead to the basement.

When he returned lugging the oxygen canister, she pointed out the door. He smiled at her, brandishing a pen-knife, and started down the stairs.

'*Ça prendre combien de temps?*' she called after him.

'How long will it take?' he yelled back. 'I'm not sure. Less than twenty minutes, I hope. Just be ready to get the hell out of here once I'm through.' He clumped noisily down the steps.

Keep busy, she thought coolly. *Do what you need to do, then be ready to go. They're dead. They can't feel a thing now. It doesn't matter anyway.*

But she still had to set this scenario up right; make it look the way it *ought* to look. *Comme il fait.*

She opened a cupboard, took out two packets of popcorn, and thrust them into the microwave before hurrying back to the O'Conners, sitting there on their recliners, arms flung out, feet akimbo.

That won't do.

As she approached the red-faced couple, their wrinkled, sagging flesh newly mottled with dark carmine blotches, something caught the corner of her eye. A carbon monoxide detector hung on the wall over a trailing umbilicus of wire leading to an outlet.

How considerate, she thought as she peered at the zero that winked in red against a narrow black rectangle set high up in the face of the monitor.

Beneath her feet, she could hear Nevin clomping about down in the basement, followed by the sound of something falling in an echoing tumble across the concrete floor. He didn't cry out, so whatever it was that had caused the sound must have been intentional.

Back in the kitchen, the microwave pinged. Time to make things cozy!

The furnace was about three meters from the wall. The distance between the furnace outlet and the safety vent leading outside was bridged by a length of metal ducting caulked with dark reddish sealant, which prevented noxious emissions from escaping into the living quarters. Nevin considered scraping off bits of the caulking, but he would need to find something to stand on while he chipped away at it, which would be time-consuming. He could instead knock down all those storage boxes

18

teetering precariously on rough shelving units along the north wall of the basement.

The falling cartons did the trick. The pipe was knocked off-center and the sealant fell away on its own, drifting like flakes of bloody snow to the slightly damp basement floor. He turned on the furnace, and the flames fed hungrily on the propane streaming in from a huge tank crouching along the south wall.

Slipping on his mask and securing the small oxygen tank to his belt, he trod the length of the off-center pipe, looking upward. Damn! Not enough sealant had fallen away to make this scenario look feasible. He'd have to go up there anyway and enlarge the fissures.

Above him, he heard Morgance walking back and forth and imagined her going from chair to chair, straightening up the couple, fixing them just so, staging them perfectly. Yes, Morgance was a perfectionist all right.

The rapid change in the blinking red numbers on the carbon monoxide monitor, which now read one hundred and fifty, took Morgance somewhat aback when she re-entered the living room, two steaming bags in her hand. She approached the seated couple, now cozily draped with the hideous orange-and-yellow afghans she'd found folded over the back of the loveseat. Ripping open the popcorn bags, she placed one on each of their laps. Ordering herself to breathe normally, not to gasp or hyperventilate, she switched on the VCR.

'And where do we hide our movies?' she asked the silent pair before trying the nearest bookcase. Ah, mostly black-and-white *noir* films from the forties, lots of musicals, and a few old westerns, the spidery titles hand-printed on the spines of each box.

Below her, Nevin was hammering against something — the pipes perhaps? Ping, ping, ping. He was obviously pissed off. She could hear him swearing, both in French and English.

The headache she was getting was only from all the tension, she told herself, glancing nervously at the CO monitor again, which now read two hundred and fifteen.

Nevin stepped down gingerly from the

chrome step-stool he'd used to reach the pipe. His hands were covered with tiny flecks of hard rubbery sealant, and they shook slightly as he folded his knife and put it back in his pocket. He hoped the CO levels upstairs weren't too high yet, but this furnace was a new one, and the blower seemed quite powerful.

He listened for a second, and heard the floorboards creak. That woman could survive on the moon, he marveled as he gave the furnace a last check, just to make sure it was firing properly.

The carbon monoxide monitor read three hundred and seventy-five.

Morgance selected a happy movie, smiling to herself as she slid the cassette out and popped it into the waiting slot. She pressed 'PLAY' and swiveled on her heels, her eyes sliding past the cozily bundled couple and along the wall, to a china cabinet near the door.

How had she missed them earlier? A display of *matryoshki*, easily a dozen complete sets.

Her head now undeniably thudding, Morgance clumsily moved toward the display case, where nesting dolls of every variety sat on glass shelves before her. Angels, traditional Russian ladies, cartoon characters; each one trailing down in size to a bowling-pin-shaped solid doll in the interior. They were hand-painted and beautifully detailed, just like those she'd shoplifted in that New York import store where Kostya had first spotted her. He'd told her the Russian name for the nesting dolls; and then, after they'd all talked a bit more at a nearby coffee bar, he'd told Morgance and Nevin just enough about the Contessa Lines caper to whet their interest.

She smiled as she reached out a flushed hand for the cabinet door latch, reflecting on the opportunity they had been given for a huge score, just because she and Kostya had wandered into the same store at the exact same moment to admire that display of little wooden nesting dolls — no, *matryoshki*. One doll inside another doll inside yet another. The significance of that image wasn't lost on her at all, not after what she and Nevin had accomplished thus far, and what they were about to accomplish in the near future.

But these dolls were *so* beautiful. Better even than the ones in New York.

We've already taken their lives, she thought. *Why not take something that has a little meaning — for me, at least?*

She carefully unlatched the cabinet doors.

As Nevin climbed the basement steps, he realized his oxygen had run out. Pulling the clinging mask away from his face, he began choking from the mounting carbon monoxide in the air. Slamming the basement door shut behind him, he sprinted through the kitchen toward the living room. He hadn't heard Morgance moving for at least two minutes.

'Oh *mon Dieu*,' he began when he caught a first glimpse of her.

She was standing so still, with her closed-lipped smile and her scarlet-flushed face, he subconsciously added her body to the count of the two already in the room. She had both hands in her coat pockets, and the tickets and passports taken from the old couple's discarded jackets were tucked inside her coat neckline, so that they stuck out over her breasts.

'Why don't you put those in your pockets?' he said as he hurried over to take her by the elbow and lead her out of the house, the TV flickering behind them, the volume turned up high as Fred Astaire danced across the screen in a Navy uniform.

But it wasn't until they were out of the house and standing on the front porch that he realized he'd left the empty oxygen tank in the O'Conners' living room.

He ran back in and waved a cheery '*Merci, adieu!*' at the still-silent couple watching a movie with blind eyes and uneaten popcorn cooling in their laps. He grabbed the tank and ran back out again, all in a matter of seconds.

Only when he was shutting the door and dead-bolting it did Morgance finally speak, her voice faint. 'I'll need to touch up the appliances, Nevin. Once I'm done, we'll have just enough time to make it to the airport.'

'Is there *that* much difference in their looks?'

'Different enough. Their faces are more

subtly colored than they looked in the pictures. I'll need to make a few . . . adjustments.' She felt more lucid now as they climbed back into the limo.

'Do you think someone might notice?' Nevin glanced at her nervously.

Settling down in the passenger seat, Morgance merely shrugged, while her fingers kneaded something in her pockets. Something that made odd clacking sounds which Nevin decided not to ask her about. Whatever she'd done in there, there was not enough time to go back and change it now.

As Morgance had said, they were on a very tight schedule.

2

' — sidence. Please leave your name and number after the beep.'

Blake Bainbridge's father's voice on the answering machine was enough to make his stomach writhe, just as it did when he heard the man in person. But before he could steady himself long enough to leave a message, Blake heard the dull click of the other receiver in the Fort Lauderdale hotel suite being picked up. And even though Amyas said nothing, he could hear her breathing as she listened — and waited.

Blake replaced the receiver, but he couldn't get the phone back on the bedside table before Amyas clacked in on skinny-heeled pumps.

'You don't have to worry,' Blake began. 'I wasn't going to tell him where we are.'

Amyas's Tabu perfume was so overpowering that Blake subconsciously edged away from her as she reached out to rest a long-nailed hand on his right arm before cooing, 'Blake. Now why would you want to contact him at all? After all that he's done and said to you, what do you owe him? Nothing. Did *he* do a thing to help you when you were . . . sick?'

'Please, Amyas.' Blake squirmed in anguish. 'Please, not again.'

'And did your father hold you and comfort you while you were recovering from that terrible accident — when you lost control of your car in the snowstorm, and nearly lost your life as well?' she queried. 'No. *Kenway* was the one who did that,' she insisted. 'And me . . . but *not your father*. He had cast you aside by then. So why crawl back to him now?'

'I . . . I just wanted to rub it in.' Blake's voice cracked. 'That's all. I just wanted to remind him to take a look at his credit cards before they were rejected. I don't think he'll forgive me for the public humiliation, but — '

'But what, love?

He hated being . . . *manipulated* like this. It was just like what his father had done to him before. *Odd*, he mused, *how*

I just can't bring myself to tell her off. But after all she's done for me, how can I? She gave me strength. All I gave her was money.

Amyas wrapped her hand around Blake's right hand and wrist, gripping him tightly. 'If he doesn't realize by now that you have his cards, why bother to tell him? And why didn't you simply ask him for them in the first place?'

'Amyas, don't. Just don't.' Blake removed her hand. 'He wouldn't have understood about Kenway,' he went on, massaging his aching leg. 'He wouldn't understand about any of this that we're doing. And I doubt he'd understand what I've found with you.'

'So then why call the man?' Amyas's voice was light and playful as she reached out to caress Blake's shoulders.

Despite her four-inch heels, her head barely reached Blake's mid-chest. He stared down at her. She seemed doll-like and delicate. But despite that, Blake knew that he would never be as strong as she was.

Especially when it came to the things

which mattered most in life: Resolve, Loyalty, a Sense of Purpose, and — most important of all — Unity, the natural result of the blending of Kenway Trumball's three Foundations in Life. Blake's father, a successful Fortune 500 executive, had never offered those things to him — the basic principles of life, which most of society ignored, or so it seemed to Blake.

So why call his father at all? He'd done the deed; followed through on his Resolve, out of Loyalty to Kenway and the rest. And thanks to his Sense of Purpose that his actions had restored in him, his 'sickness' had been conquered. Which led to Unity; and making late-night calls to his father about the stolen credit cards had nothing whatsoever to do with Kenway's Foundation. Nothing at all.

It was done only for spite.

Yes. That was it. He merely wanted to rub salt into the old, festering wounds.

Staring down into Amyas's eyes, Blake felt a rush of gratitude toward this woman, toward her mentor Kenway, and

— most of all — towards the Foundation.

Bending down to kiss the top of her forehead, Blake murmured, 'Don't mention this to Kenway, will you? I know how he feels about his privacy.'

Now the scent of Tabu was a live thing in his nostrils. Amyas brought her lips up close to his and whispered, her breath heavy with the herbal fragrance of the yerba mate tea she drank daily, 'Silly. Why should I speak to him of this? Displeasing Kenway at such a crucial time would be . . . what is the term? Counter-productive?'

Blake nodded. Their lips met. He held her tighter, then tighter still, until it seemed that theirs was a single body, twin hearts beating in steady Unity.

★   ★   ★

Later, lying in the darkness next to Amyas, listening to her gentle breathing close to his ear, Blake fought the need to answer nature's call for as long as possible, lest he wake her. Finally, he painfully got out of bed, his knee stiff and aching under the tight elastic bandage.

Despite all her understanding, she still could not bear to look at his mangled leg. And out of his appreciation for her presence, he'd acquiesced to all of her admittedly small demands: disrobing out of her sight, making love in total darkness, and wearing the compression wrap at all times, especially on the flight down from New York.

By making use of his misfortune and his deformity, however, he had proven himself to Kenway, and he had finally been accepted as an asset to the Foundation's coming Goal.

As he made his way to the bathroom he passed by the window and looked out towards Port Everglades, where the cruise ship *Nerissa*, the culmination of their Goal, was docked in readiness for tomorrow's cruise.

He peered down from his fifth-story vantage at the distant Atlantic. Moonlight frosted the choppy, rippling waves, reminding Blake of the snow they'd left back in New York City that morning. But once the thought of snow crossed his mind, other less appealing images followed, and he quitted the window and hurried on to answer more pressing needs.

Blake glanced at his reflection in the mirror above the vanity and leaned closer to examine his visage more carefully. He disliked looking at his face, even though he was considered good-looking, handsome even. He had never been particularly fond of his looks to begin with; much less so after the accident. Not that he had been disfigured in any way. The imploded airbag had prevented that.

No. What Blake disliked was how his close resemblance to his father had intensified with the proliferation of worry lines that now scored his forehead and cheeks. His father had the exact same furrows in his face, albeit deeper-etched amid the rest of the age-related wrinkles. But Blake was only thirty years old. No man his age deserved a face such as the one he wore now.

Blake closed his pain-drawn eyes and took a shaky breath. He could hear Amyas's slow, regular breathing in the other room. If he closed the bathroom door, then *very* quietly stepped into the adjoining salon, she couldn't hear him dial the phone there, could she?

From memory he punched in the string of numbers, listening for Amyas's footsteps. But as soon as the phone in his father's house began ringing, Blake no longer cared if she was listening or not.

'You have reached the Blake Bainbridge residence. Please leave your name and number after the beep. Someone will get back to you. Thank you.'

Blake bit his lip as his father's voice died out and the beep sounded. The message had been so quintessentially Blake Bainbridge, *père*. The tacit sense of control; of domination.

Blake paused, gripped by a sense of utter helplessness. What in the world *did* he intend to say?

'Uhm . . . The *Nerissa*. Tomorrow. I, uhm . . . goodbye.'

Replacing the receiver back on its base, Blake closed his eyes. *He will have no idea what I was referring to*, he told himself. *Even if he figures some of it out, he has no idea of the real Goal. Let him wonder about it all. Oh God! Why did he have to sound so much like me?*

The memory of his father's pronounced upper-class accent over the phone line echoed in Blake's head. Just as the memory of his own words now reverberated in his consciousness.

What he'd done indicated that, contrary to his earlier smugness, he had no Resolve, no Loyalty, and even worse, no Sense of Purpose. His actions defied the whole concept of Unity; but yet . . .

'He was my father, before Kenway. I was born to him.'

Blake's voice was a plaintive, aching whisper in the darkness of the suite's sitting room.

And if his call had wakened Amyas, she had chosen not to acknowledge his lapse in judgment.

★   ★   ★

'Looks like you folks are in luck — there's a baggage check-in kiosk at the terminal entrance. They'll take care of everything for you there,' the cabbie said, as he slowed to a stop before the front entrance

34

of the airline that would be flying Mr. and Mrs. Norman O'Conner to Fort Lauderdale. The elderly couple had been a pleasure to drive in from their hotel in Des Plaines. All through their journey to O'Hare International Airport in Chicago, they had sat quietly and didn't ask a lot of dumb questions.

'That's wonderful,' the old lady gushed, her voice unnaturally high and girlish.

'Saves us a hike to the ticket counter, eh, Mildred?' her husband wheezed.

'You know 'bout them electronic trams, dontcha?' the taxi driver added. 'If they don't offer you folks one, just ask, OK?'

Enthusiastic nods from the diminutive couple confirmed that they would.

'That'll be thirty-two twenty-five.'

'And you keep the change, son,' the old man rasped after he'd handed over a crisp fifty-dollar bill.

Hey, thanks!' The cabbie happily pocketed the generous tip and got out to unload their luggage.

Norman slid clumsily out of the back seat and turned to help his wife out. The driver led them over to the nearby kiosk and got them safely settled in line before heading out for his next fare.

Taking a final glance out the window, the cabbie watched as they checked in and pocketed their claim tickets.

What a nice old couple. Wish all my fares were like that, he thought as he pulled away from the airline's bustling front entrance.

★   ★   ★

The cabbie was right. The airline rep behind the kiosk counter took one look at the approaching O'Conners, both decidedly decrepit and short of breath from the brief walk into the airport, and routinely called for two wheelchairs.

During the brief, bumpy ride from the kiosk to the concourse, the attendants half-running, weaving from side to side like football players to avoid pedestrians, the couple sat beaming with excitement as the wheelchairs hummed along beneath them. They were whisked to the upper level on a service elevator, then wheeled to a smooth stop at the checkpoint.

Solemnly they offered up their tickets and identification to the TSA agent in charge. Norman fished the little card out of his wallet that stated he had an implanted pacemaker, which did not allow him to go through the metal detector.

After a cursory glance at the photos, then back at the couple, the agent motioned for them to stay seated in their chairs as his partner shoved their carry-on bags through the X-ray scanner. He took another quick glance at their IDs. 'No need to take off your shoes folks,' he said. 'Age has its advantages, don't it? Just ride on over to the gate; the attendants will assist you on the other side. Have a safe trip, Mr. and Mrs. O'Conner. Be sure to enjoy yourselves in Fort Lauderdale,' he added as an afterthought.

The X-ray scanner attendant shoved their bags through the machine, detecting only dense layers of old-people crap — prescription pill bottles and tubes of God knew what, all properly labeled and contained, as required, in three-ounce portions in plastic ziplock baggies. She wagged a finger at her partner as the

O'Conners were helped aboard an electric tram and put-putted off toward their boarding gate. 'Now what if they actually *were* terrorists, huh?' she chuckled.

Snorting, her partner replied, 'Oh yeah, like *they're* gonna ring all the cherries on the terrorist meter.' He turned his attention back to the remaining bleary-eyed passengers at the scanning station.

Not only did this couple *not* fit the profile, but he doubted they'd even notice they were all but alone on this particular flight, let alone try to plot ways to sabotage it.

★　★　★

First class was all but deserted on the red-eye to Fort Lauderdale; most of the passengers who did board the plane after the O'Conners were seated back in tourist. And true to the prediction of the young man who'd cheerfully waved them past the metal detector, the elderly couple from Barrington had the entire front of the plane to themselves that morning.

'I hope our 'employers' have everything

ready for us,' Nevin whispered as he took delicate sips of champagne through the set of artificial tooth-caps snapped in place over his own teeth, leaving a creased swipe of reddish lipstick on the rim of the plastic glass.

'Kostya assured me everything is in place,' Morgance replied. 'His people want this to work just as badly as we do. After all the trouble they've gone through, I don't think they'll be inclined to back out now. Besides, think of what we've saved them by using the O'Conners — proper cruise tickets in hand, bags with appropriate clothing already packed, legitimate IDs in order. The good IDs alone would've been difficult to obtain on short notice.'

'So now we're no more than faux people, *non*?' Nevin mused.

'*Au contraire, mon ami*. I've never felt more *real* in all my life,' she shot back before settling comfortably in her seat for the trip. She eyed the unfamiliar visage that stared back at her from the black mirror of glass at her side: Norman O'Conner, recently deceased. *And* alive and well. '*Fait accompli*,' she whispered to her/himself; then thought, *Norman est mort, vive le Norman!* while recalling with satisfaction the *tableau mort* they'd left behind in Barrington Hills.

★ ★ ★

Exiting a short dead-end road on the outskirts of a suburb not far from the Greater Pittsburgh International Airport, David Spaulding pulled into the circular driveway in front of Conrad Emerson's colonial-style tract house. Mentally he matched the cars parked outside to the people waiting inside. Carl and Rachel Frick's immaculate Ford was snuggled next to Chip and Doreen Lutz's dusty old Chevy.

'Hell,' he grumbled, pulling in next to Chip, 'they're here already. I can just imagine what — and who — they've been talking about in there.'

'In front of Connie? I doubt it.' Deb got out of the car. 'C'mon babe, they know how much he cares about you. Who was sitting front and center in the courtroom every day of the hearing? He's more of a father to you than your own dad was. And you know it.'

David slammed his door shut with a whumping thud that echoed in the chilly morning air. 'We'll see who's right once the guilty silence descends.' He sprinted up the porch steps and rang the bell while Deb trotted to join him.

'I was just wondering where you kids were,' came Connie's dry chuckle as he pulled open the double oak doors with a courtly flourish and beamed at each of them in turn. His dark blue suit was stylishly dapper, and he proudly sported cuff-links bearing miniature Pittsburgh Police Department emblems. Leaning down, his silvery-white hair and pale blue eyes gleaming, he gave both a quick hug, then ushered them in.

'The others are having 'pick-me-ups' in the front parlor,' he said somewhat apologetically, 'but I doubt we'll have time for another round before we go. I hope you kids already ate.'

'Does this mean we've been picked as designated drivers?' David asked. 'I don't know if I can handle a minivan full of drunken cops and their women this early in the morning.' He winked at his long-time mentor. Deborah was right of course. Connie was definitely more like a father to him than his own had been — their temperaments and tastes were so similar.

And, much like an affectionate father, Connie reached over and ruffled David's hair as the three of them headed down the oak-floored hallway toward the old-fashioned parlor. 'You nailed me, kiddo,' he admitted. 'Another dastardly plan foiled by the copper.'

'Hey, Dave,' came Chip's slightly boozy greeting. 'You made me lose five bucks, you dumb cluck. I bet Carl that you and Deb would wanna go somewhere cold instead of to the tropics — you're already 'roasting' here in Pittsburgh, ya know.'

'What did I tell you?' David whispered through clenched teeth into Deborah's ear.

'Nah. I knew you wasn't about to forfeit your deposit,' Carl chimed in. 'You've been outta work for too many months already.'

Next to Carl on the loveseat, his wife Rachel whispered loudly to him, 'Hush Carl, you're *embarrassing* them.'

Chip interrupted her. 'I guess the old saw's right. When you're hot, you're — '

'Chip, stick a cork in it,' Doreen snapped. She shot him an exasperated glare.

'Now, now,' Connie interjected. 'The boys are just letting off steam.' He leaned in closer to David. 'This whole situation was rough on them, too, kiddo. The hearing, the whole mess with the auditors — what happened to you affected all of them as well. Everyone's been on edge since the damned consent decree was shoved down the force's throat by the Justice Department. Not much they can do to let off tension besides griping about things in general.'

'But just wait'll we're on the *Nerissa*, my boy,' Connie added. 'They'll all settle down and enjoy themselves. You'll see, kiddo. It's gonna be a happy, restful trip for — '

Suddenly, the sound of a horn outside caught their attention. Connie turned away from David and Deb to announce: 'Ladies and gentlemen, our chariot has arrived. I took the liberty of requesting a shuttle from the airport. You can all leave your cars parked here; they'll be perfectly safe.'

As they began to move out to their cars to collect their various bags and belongings, Connie remained close to Dave and Deb, as if to say to the others, 'Back off — the kid's with *me*.'

And for just this once, David Spaulding was grateful to be the object of such a protective, *fatherly* gesture.

3

'*Nevin!* Wake up!'

'Yeah, yeah, awake,' Nevin mumbled, swinging his legs over the side of the bed before cradling his face in his hands. His cheeks were still sticky from the gummy adhesive Morgance had applied last night to secure the squishy-soft fleshy appliance to his face.

They'd pulled off their disguises and stripped to their underwear to catch some sleep after arriving from the airport in Fort Lauderdale earlier that morning, and now Morgance was up and dressed in her own clothes. Her 'Norman' clothes were laid out on the still-made bed, though: the dark suit, the rumpled shirt and tie, the breast-binder that hid her bosom, and the broadcloth and spandex filler she'd fashioned to mimic a squat old man's sagging body.

'Nevin, are you going to sit there in your underwear, or are you going to put something on?' She folded the stretchy white female body-shaper she'd made for him and placed it on the foot of his bed, where she'd already laid out a woman's pants suit and flowered blouse taken from Mildred's packed suitcase.

'Think that'll fit me?' The old woman had seemed very tiny to him.

'It will once I fix it.' Morgance gestured to him. 'Come on. At least put on a pair of pants. These people will be insulted if you aren't dressed.'

'*These people* are criminals, *n'est-ce pas?*'

'*N'importe,*' she replied, shrugging.

Nevin wriggled into his jeans, then stared at his reflection in the mirror over the dresser. The dark circles were back under his eyes, and in the room's indirect lighting his cheeks looked sunken. At least Morgance's appliances, disgusting as they might feel, hid some of the ravages of his having had only a few hours of sleep since they'd left Québec three days ago.

Three knocks at the door, then a pause, followed by two more knocks.

Nevin didn't need to turn around to

see the four men enter the motel room and greet Morgance. Reflected in the mirror, they were an incongruous lot — one man thin, perhaps twenty-five years of age; the other three somewhat older and heavier. They were all neatly groomed and well-dressed in lightweight summer-style jackets and slacks. Not at all what one might picture when the words 'Russian Mafia' were uttered.

'*Dõbry dyen*,' one of the older men said. 'Hi, kids.' The young man followed close behind him with a pair of leather suitcases with security straps.

Morgance echoed the greeting, the Russian sounding odd in her native Canadian accent, while motioning for them to make themselves comfortable around a small table near the window. The older men took seats while the young man continued to stand.

One man, with close-cropped iron-gray hair, seemed to be in charge. He spoke in slightly accented but impeccable English. 'I'm glad to see your first objective has been met. Arranging for the O'Conners to win that cruise line vacation with all

47

expenses paid was a cinch for us, with our connections.'

He glanced over at the facial appliances set out on a towel laid across the dresser top and nodded in approval. The resemblance to the O'Conner ID photos was uncanny, if slightly morbid. Morgance had used her skills with the airbrush and texturing tools to good advantage.

'And everything else in Illinois has been taken care of, just as we promised.' She smiled at them. 'So now, I'm assuming that *your* first objective has been met also?'

The man sitting next to Close-cropped nodded. 'The first half of your fee is waiting in *Shvĕstkayă bănkă smĕtkă* — one half for each of you — and will be moved to your Swiss account later today. The second half will be added to that once the final objective has been met. But until then, perhaps we might go over the general plan? Mr. Marmion, is that agreeable with you?' he asked suddenly, looking over at Nevin, who was still standing in front of the mirror with his back to the others.

The young man waiting next to their luggage whispered, '*Kăk ŏn?* — What's with him?'

Morgance walked over to Nevin and put her arm around his bare waist before apologizing. 'He's driven hundreds of miles with very little sleep. Please forgive his rudeness.' She gave his midriff a painful squeeze, then narrowed her eyes at him.

Nevin forced himself to smile as he turned around to their guests, saying, 'Terribly sorry . . . Yes, please, let's go over the plans again.'

Morgance quietly positioned herself near the door. They had given instructions at the desk that they wouldn't be leaving until later in the afternoon, but housekeeping still might show up unannounced.

In spite of his fatigue, Nevin forced himself to listen intently as Close-cropped began to speak. 'Depending on your ability to infiltrate the area we've discussed, it might become necessary to create a bit of chaos prior to the

49

execution of your ultimate task. If such diversions become necessary . . . ' He turned to the young man guarding the cases. 'Levka?'

Levka picked up a bag and placed it on the round table. He opened it to reveal two Kevlar vests surrounded by several plastic-wrapped devices, complete with timers and detonators. The explosives were small, but potentially lethal, should one be standing too close when they were detonated. The timers were small enough to fit into a pocket or purse, and the controls were simple enough to manipulate sight unseen — a plus, since avoiding undue attention was essential to their plan.

'What's the range?' Morgance asked.

They could be many yards away from the charges while safely detonating them, Levka assured her, regardless of whether or not walls were between them and their targeted site.

While the men discussed the finer points of the explosives with Morgance, Nevin examined the Kevlar vests. For such seemingly benign garments — black, shiny synthetic fabric with hard segments of padding sealed within — the mere sight of them, nonetheless, made his flesh crawl. The implication behind their very need was unsettling. True, it was mostly a contingency item, designed as protection against the explosives. But another possibility lingered in Nevin's mind.

We just might get shot. Someone might shoot us, and then we'll need these things. Of course, they have security on the ship. They have a casino on board; must be lots of cash floating about. They'd have to have beefed up security for that, wouldn't they?

He came out of his reverie. 'Levka, the other case,' Close-cropped was saying.

The second bag was brought to the table and opened to reveal night-vision goggles, surveillance equipment, and climbing gear.

Odd. Nevin had no idea what they would use the climbing gear for. Must be yet another contingency item, in case their in-ship path to their ultimate destination within the bowels of the *Nerissa* was blocked.

One thing he did notice: everything was Russian Army issue, and was far superior to anything he had seen either in the States or Canada. Yes, Nevin mused, this would all do quite well when they needed to gain access to the ship's satellite system. And with the climbing equipment, they could even enter the room from outside the ship if need be.

'Looks good,' Morgance said. 'This operation is a definite 'go,' gentlemen. And I understand that our contact on the *Nerissa* will meet us as we board?'

'Yes — Kostya Varvarinski. Officially, he's serving as one of the pursers,' Close-cropped said with a nod. 'And he'll be on the lookout for your arrival. Once you're on board, you can begin implementing the plan — when you're well out to sea, of course. Gentlemen,' he said, turning to the others, 'it's time to leave. Remember,' he added to Morgance, 'the second half of your fee will be paid only upon proof of completion of your final task. We'll be watching — and waiting, so you two . . . *do good*.' He spoke his conclusion with a smile that almost made it up to his eyes, before he and his companions quitted the room, shutting the door softly behind them.

Once they were gone, Morgance hurried over to the set of appliances they'd used the night before and picked up the pieces she'd soon be wearing. 'You'd better shave. We have less than two hours to get dressed and into make-up, and hide all that stuff in the cases with some of our own clothes.'

Nevin found himself shivering at the thought of the O'Conners' garments as 'our own' clothes.

$$\star \quad \star \quad \star$$

Rachel clutched her stomach as the vacation group from Pittsburgh deplaned from their flight to Fort Lauderdale's Hollywood International Airport. Behind her, Carl and Chip were pretending not to have felt the effects of the flight, despite their wan complexions and shivering chins.

But Doreen didn't seem affected by either the slightly turbulent flight or their cramped tourist-class seating. She and Chip were continuing the spat they'd begun two weeks earlier. Chip had insisted they go on the cruise with his pals, while Doreen had wanted to use the money to get their house improved.

As their group staggered into the terminal, Connie said, 'You watch. The ones who are moaning about being air-sick will suddenly exchange that for sea-sickness. Care to bet who'll make it to dinner tonight?'

Dave nodded. 'The ones I want to see hanging their heads over the porcelain altar are Chip and Carl. Damn, isn't anyone from the cruise line coming to pick up our luggage? I don't see their repre — '

Connie patted Dave's shoulder, chuckling. 'Patience, my boy. Or we could sue the cruise line — you could buy a brand-new wardrobe on the ship. Did you realize they have the equivalent of a mini-mall on board?'

'Not to mention a wedding chapel,' Deb broke in from the window seat.

Connie laughed. 'Look, our patience has paid off — there's the Contessa rep now. No need to stop at the mall after all.'

'Or the wedding chapel.' Chip had come up behind them brandishing his carry-on bag like a shield. David bared his teeth and shook a fist at Chip in exasperation.

The uniformed Contessa Lines representative waited for the bags bearing the cruise line's special tags to make their appearance on the slow-moving luggage carousel.

Connie's voice burbled with enthusiasm a few seconds later when he announced to their group, 'Ride's here — c'mon, kids, we're goin' sailing!'

Wishing he could muster even half the older man's energy, David followed Connie as the retired cop strode jauntily out of the terminal with Deb holding on to his proffered arm. They moved toward the waiting blue-and-gold-painted shuttles as the Contessa rep assured everyone that their large bags would be sent on ahead to the ship and would be waiting in their cabins.

Chip joined David. 'What's up Dave?' he asked. 'A lovers' tiff?'

'Who're you?' Spaulding shot back without missing a beat. 'An idiot cop with nose problems?'

He quickened his pace to catch up with Deborah, who was climbing aboard the first of the four shuttles waiting at the curb. Connie was already seated toward the middle of the vehicle's ten rows of seats. As the two sat down across the narrow aisle from him, he leaned over and said, 'Come, come, you two. I didn't spend all this moola and fly everyone this far just to look at frowning faces. You're on vacation, kids! Pittsburgh's half a continent away and freezing its cajones off. Enjoy! Kiss, make up. Only don't make out, OK? Save it for the stateroom.' Deb sighed. 'Promise I won't mention that place on the ship again — at least not until we're finally out to sea. OK, babe?'

Dave waited until Chip was safely seated toward the front of the shuttle, well out of earshot, before reaching over to squeeze her hand. 'Just so long as you make sure it's only a day or so,' he said with a smile.

The shuttle doors closed and the driver

switched on the engine and pulled away from the curb.

At last they were off to Port Everglades and the waiting *Nerissa*.

★ ★ ★

Richard Black Wolf, eyes squinting behind his sunglasses, unbuttoned his jacket in the blistering Port Everglades Florida sun.

Janice would love this, he thought. *The sun, the damned heat, the smell of salt, the people . . . Well, it's her loss, not mine. All I lost was her. But damn, I got me some sun and a whole lot of hot weather — couple of things I can't stand; but here I am, baking and sweating and wishing to God I was back in San Francisco. And Janice is probably still bitching to whoever'll listen how chilly and rainy San Fran is for her. Somehow, something doesn't add up here.*

'Richard? Oh great, it *is* you,' came Martin Abbot's cheerful greeting as the agent joined his client, a tape-strapped box in hand.

Sliding his sunglasses down his nose,

Richard snorted. 'Aw come *on*, Marty. Who the hell else would it be? Like you know a bunch of tattooed, pony-tailed Amerindian guys with no tolerance for the heat.'

'Hey, man, it's Florida. You see all kinds of folks here.' Abbott paused to wipe the sweat off his face, then continued. 'Anyway, I was hoping I'd catch you before the ship left port. This came in to my office yesterday.' He gestured at the box. 'And since I intended to say goodbye in person anyhow . . . '

Giving his client a weak smile and a shrug of his well-padded shoulders, the literary agent held out the rectangular box, shipping label facing Richard. He immediately recognized that steeply forward-slanting block printing. Just what he needed — another reminder of Janice.

'You made sure the airline X-rayed it, right?' Leaning forward, he took the box from Marty's hands and set it on his knee, while he continued to lean against the rental car.

His agent laughed. 'Would you believe they tested it with that trace detector

58

analysis gizmo? Rubbed the whole thing with something that looked like a coffee filter, then popped that into some kind of black plastic toaster-thing to see if it was a bomb! When you *see* what was actually in there in the first scan they did . . . '

Richard nodded. He'd been through enough airports during his last book tour to know what Marty meant by the coffee-filter/plastic-toaster gizmo. He even knew the name of the other scanner they'd used: the CTX 5000. Just as he'd watched his carry-on bags go through the scanners in over a dozen major airports.

Supposedly the more detailed scans were done at random because of a shortage of machines dealing with an ever-increasing number of passengers flying each day. But somehow, for some unknown reason, *his* bags wound up being multi-scanned every damn time. Janice used to say it was because Richard was 'high-profile' or some crap like that. But that made absolutely no sense to him. It wasn't as if a guy who had been on *The Tonight Show* half a dozen times should be considered a threat.

Then again, he told himself, *I suppose they don't get too many Native American anthropologists coming through the terminal. They must never know what to expect from me.*

' . . . guess they thought something might be in it, you know,' Marty was saying, 'the way drug smugglers put stuff in.'

Richard adjusted his sunglasses at the top of his nose and closed his eyes, wishing he could pull in the outsides of his ears, too, and completely shut off Marty's gibberish. Not that he disliked the guy; it wasn't his fault he was a nervous ball of energy. It was just the way his agent felt compelled to *explain* everything, be it obscure or obvious. Probably a trait he had picked up after having someone like Richard for a client for the last eleven years.

'Suppose you're going to do *this* book in long-hand and drive the editor totally nuts.'

'They didn't like my typing the last time?' Richard opened his eyes and stared his agent down.

Martin Abbott crossed his arms and sighed. 'They thought little things like margins and indenting the paragraphs would be considerate. Not that they couldn't scan what you had done, but I was asked if you'd at least *consider* using the computer this time.'

'Just as long as I can type on it with one finger,' Richard laughed, holding up his right hand with all but one of his fingers curled into his palm.

Marty rolled his eyes. 'I think you've been studying anthropology too long, Richard. Working among the river-dwellers spoiled your appreciation for progress. You *do* own a TV, don't you?'

'Of course. The only problem is, sometimes the wads of foil fall off the ends of the rabbit ears and I can't get PBS.'

'I should know better than to ask you a simple question — although I'll bet the read-out on your VCR is still blinking at twelve o'clock.'

Richard chose to ignore the jibe and began bouncing the light brown box on one jeans-covered knee, until the agent finally took the bait.

'Uh, Richard, I wouldn't do that. The thing in there won't survive if you drop it.'

'Don't tell me, Janice sent something alive in a box with no air holes punched in it.'

''Survive' as in 'fragile.' Look at the stickers. Richard,' Marty continued tentatively, 'I know how you feel about e-mail, but this ship really does have full online capacity — complete satellite access, all the latest doodads. So would it be asking too much for you to send your editor a line or two while you're on board? I know they want to keep abreast of your progress on the new book.'

'No. You know why they want to keep their thumbs planted squarely in the middle of my back,' Richard said without any particular malice. 'Just like you know how much I hate to email anybody from anywhere, especially a cruise ship.' He paused to wipe the sweat from his face again before going on. 'Who knows *what* happens to that message, or how many people might get a look at it — intercept it, even — before it finally makes it to New York? C'mon Marty. I've done five books with them. They know how I operate.'

The agent shook his head, his eyes squinting against the reflected brilliance of the winter sun over the choppy water beyond Richard's parked rental car. He paused to scratch the tip of his nose. 'I don't think I've ever known anyone who was so open about virtually every detail of his life, yet at the same time so enigmatic, so *closed*. All I'm trying to say is, the editor *and* the publisher would very much appreciate it if you'd come up for air once in a while and at least talk to them *before* the entire book comes to them typed in a box, instead of electronically, like everyone else's.'

Richard propped a booted heel on the curb. 'Here's the way it works, Marty. I give you a proposal. You submit it. They buy it. Then I write it, and you deliver the completed work. *Everyone* knows what to expect — don't they?'

'All right,' Marty conceded. 'But I was told they'd like to see a bit more content, and a little less of you.' He paused and stretched before continuing.

Richard didn't answer but looked away instead toward the docked *Nerissa*. He wondered if any of the people who bought his books might book passage on a cruise ship — fourteen decks worth of hedonism and self-indulgence. And at least two of those decks had been gutted of their staterooms to make way for a pair of brand-new gambling casinos. Yet another way for the Contessa Line — which often sailed half-empty these days — to carve out a profitable niche for itself, once the novelty of spending endless days at sea amidst an anonymous mass of humanity wore off.

He sighed. And now here he was, rubbing elbows with all the other tourists. All because his editor had hinted to him that the publisher would be very 'happy' if his latest book had some 'cross-over' potential into the world of pop psychology. Apparently, he was told, as the economy tanked, more and more people had become addicted to gambling, and Richard's anthropological take on the whole phenomenon might actually land him on the bestseller lists this time — or so Marty was hoping. So he was to stick to the subject of casino gambling in all its forms, and forget about all the rest of it.

He took a deep breath of briny-warm air. *OK,* he thought, *you guys win . . . up to a point. I'll make the damned book 'accessible.' Dumb it down if I have to. But nobody's going to make me enjoy it.*

Hugging the sun-warmed cardboard box close to his chest, he listened to Marty going on and on about their 'casino-culture' project.

Richard suddenly realized exactly why he'd insisted on booking passage on the *Nerissa,* the very least of the so-called 'floating casinos.' This ship was the antithesis of all the elements most people were seeking. It was conducive to solitude, rather than open to interpersonal possibilities. And its atmosphere was very unlikely to attract anyone with a mindset akin to his.

★ ★ ★

65

In their Fort Lauderdale hotel, Amyas was packing the last of their bags when Blake entered. Without looking up from the opened case on their rumpled bed, she asked, 'Was there enough left on the card to pay for the room service?'

As she spoke, Blake looked down at the credit card, a Platinum Visa: his father's card, with a dizzyingly high limit which, thank God, he hadn't quite exhausted yet. 'Yeah, everything went through just fine,' he muttered, slipping the card back into his wallet. Blake didn't want to know what the remaining balance was. As long as it was enough to cover the cost of the phone calls to his father's house last night plus their room service, he was content to remain ignorant of the severity of this latest assault on his father's credit rating.

'Do you think we'll have time to rent a car?' Amyas latched the case shut with a sharp, decisive snap of metal against metal before glancing over at him.

The room's natural light turned her hair into a nimbus around her exotic face. Blake wanted so much to pull down the disheveled sheets again and simply lie there with her; not making love, but merely creating a *moment* with her, apart from Kenway and the Foundation, and separate from all the plans and tasks of the last couple of weeks.

'Blake!' A hint of condescension underscored her carefully enunciated words. 'Have we time to rent a car?' She went on, her voice softer, more placating. 'I was only thinking that it will be so far for us to walk with these cases, and we'd have no privacy in a cab.'

'Do you have everything packed?' he asked, ignoring her question. 'The stuff in the bathroom?'

She nodded. 'But the car . . . ?'

He put his arm around her shoulder, adding, 'I'll see to it. Don't mind me; I'll be OK once we're on the ship.'

Amyas reached over to gently squeeze his right knee and the bandage there. Blake held his breath; the worst of the pain had subsided months ago, but he still disliked being touched there like that.

Amyas squeezed again, harder, before smiling at him. 'Then I suppose we're ready, *once you call for the car.*'

Kenway might have called the first principle Resolve, but Amyas managed to approach obsession in her single-minded Sense of Purpose.

* * *

It wasn't until the car arrived at the hotel that Blake began to feel fresh misgivings. Taking a cab would have been more anonymous, less memorable, than arranging for a car to be delivered to the hotel. And cheaper by far. The Visa card had to be on the verge of maxing out.

But he put their bags in the back seat, opened the passenger door for Amyas, then entered the driver's side, allowing himself to sink down into the plush leather bucket seat. He had loved to drive before the accident, but now he felt queasy each time he crossed his chest with the shoulder harness. The sensation of being trapped instead of strapped in was too real.

'Blake?'

'Huhm?' He slipped the key into the ignition.

'You do remember what Kenway told us about not seeming too *different*, once we're on the ship?'

Blake nodded, his hand still holding the key. 'I remember.' He had been gauche enough to question Kenway's decisions about their clothing. Rather than his own tastefully tailored suits, the guru had ordered them to don off-the-rack separates from strip-mall outlets, hypnotically dull in their sedate, mundane lack of style and pretentiousness.

'No one expects a tourist to come aboard carrying a gun,' Kenway had insisted. 'We must not attract too much attention until the time is right.'

But hadn't Kenway also stressed what a special role Blake would play in the Foundation? How his very *uniqueness* called for some extraordinary sacrifices on his part, just to balance out his attributes against the others' lack of them?

It was all part of the Goal, the Big Picture, he'd been assured.

And right now the only thing standing in the way of achieving that Goal was the simple turn of a key in an ignition.

As he stared past the car hood toward the not-so-distant Port Everglades and the sparkling *Nerissa* waiting in her berth, Kenway's words echoed in his mind with the harshness of gunshots: *No one expects a tourist to come aboard carrying a gun . . . No one expects . . .*

Kenway was right: no one would suspect him; no one would question him. So then why did his stomach feel like it was weighed down with lead? Why did his heart pound so painfully?

Because even I wouldn't expect this of myself, came the troubling counterpoint to Kenway's remembered words.

He bit his lower lip and with the simple twist of his key in the ignition, put the Foundation's timetable into motion.

4

David had been a superstitious man. He would have hailed a taxi fifteen minutes ago to head back to the airport, but he'd given up on believing in omens — bad, good or indifferent — months ago, during that fatal night in the projects.

So while the Contessa Lines shuttle's engine steamed and sputtered, and his fellow riders stood agitated and sweating alongside the stalled vehicle, David leaned against a street-lamp base and re-read the brochure attached to his boarding pass and cabin assignment:

'Welcome to the *Nerissa*!'

'Unlike the mega-liners whose larger size equals increased opportunities for missed connections, the *Nerissa* offers the best of the sea-going worlds: A spacious layout, combined with a closer passenger/crew ratio.

Need to find a certain dining room, or that special hideaway? All corridors feature easy-to-read maps, not only of your own deck, but cut-away displays of the entire ship for your convenience.'

'Which is just another way of saying, 'We've downsized our passenger capacity, but we're still stuck with a damned big ship.'' David looked up, startled. Chip was standing next to him and reading over his shoulder.

'Hey, didn't mean to spook you,' Chip went on. 'I was just talking to Connie and he said this ship used to carry over a thousand passengers. Before they went niche and shoved in those casinos, to make them more money.'

David glanced over at the others. Connie and Deborah were off to one side having an earnest discussion about something or other. Doreen and Rachel were talking to some women near the front of the shuttle, and Carl was hunkered down on the curb next to the shuttle, chatting up their driver.

'Who are those women the girls are talking to?' queried David. 'They seem to be having quite a conversation.'

'Over there?' Dave nodded. 'They seem to be involved with some weird cult called the Foundation.'

Chip didn't seem happy about it.

'So what *is* bugging you, Chip? What's going on with you?'

Chip scratched his head before speaking again. 'I'm so sick and tired of being ignored by Doreen. Y'know? Strangers I can take. But when it's the people I'm closest to, then it gets to me. It really does. Like, would it kill her to talk to *me* instead of those weirdos? Hell, I don't need this.'

David shook his head. 'You mean those women over there? What's the big deal? After all, Deb's talking to Connie, not me, but do you see me worrying about it?' Wincing as he realized how mean he sounded, he quickly added, 'And if it's the rest of us you're steamed at, then hell, it's a big ship. There will be other people on board, I can guarantee you that. Just give it a shot.'

'Shut up, Spaulding,' Chip whined. 'You don't know nothin' about what's going on between Doreen and me.'

I really don't need this right now, David told himself, shoving his brochure under one arm and putting the other around Chip's shoulder. 'Look,' he said more gently. 'Listen to me. I'm saying this to you as a friend, OK? You want to muck about in your own self-pity, then have at it. That's fine with me. But right now I'd be more than happy to trade my problems for yours. So either pick yourself up and take what this ship has to offer with gratitude, or hail yourself a cab back to the airport and haul your sorry butt back to Pittsburgh. And just be thankful,' he added with a growl, 'that the FBI isn't going through all *your* records. Right now what you're going through doesn't look all that bad to me, given all the crap *I've* had to swallow the last few months. Now go talk to Carl, or just go somewhere — anywhere — else.'

Chip's eyes had widened in surprise as David talked and were now staring, unblinking, at his former partner. He pulled away, muttering, 'Sorry. It's just so damned hot out here . . . and my head hurts . . . and when the hell is that shuttle going to get moving?'

★　★　★

David didn't notice when Carl got up off the curb until he heard the cop's voice. 'They're sending another shuttle from Contessa,' he said to Connie and Deborah. 'Should be another five or ten minutes, max.'

'Dave,' Connie called to him.

Reluctantly he lifted his eyes away from the sunbaked concrete at his feet and looked over at his mentor.

'Carl says the cavalry's on its way with replacements.'

'Okay, I'm coming,' David said.

But he found he was reluctant to move from this spot. He watched Deb board the stalled shuttle and haul out their bags. He should go help her, but he felt frozen in time, like a fly caught in amber. He didn't want to move for anything, and somehow even a small amount of effort seemed beyond him.

'Kiddo,' Connie said, placing a firm hand on his left shoulder and giving it a warming squeeze, 'I overheard what you said to Chip. I can't honestly say I blame you. But all that talk about the FBI watching you is just that — talk. Do you actually think you would have been allowed to go on this little jaunt if it was all that serious? They would have descended on you like a tornado on Kansas, my boy, if they thought you were a risk for flight. It's been weeks since the hearing. If they had anything at all, they'd have sprung it by now.'

For the first time in the twenty years he'd been a cop, David Spaulding suddenly wished that Conrad Emerson would leave him the hell alone.

'Hey, guys.' Carl's deep voice cut through the hubbub of the busy thoroughfare. 'It's coming. Let's get aboard.'

David followed Connie onto the waiting shuttle silently, not even bothering to see if Deb had gotten all their bags on or not. All he wanted to do right now was sit down and zone out on the short ride to the dock.

But Deb couldn't leave it alone either. 'Don't worry, I got our bags. Sounded like you were pissed at Chip, so I thought — '

'I'm fine,' he snapped a little too quickly.

The shuttle driver hit the ignition and the engine burst into life. Deb tried again. 'Connie was telling me all about the last time he was on one of these ships, and how different everything seems now,' she rattled on. 'He read an article about how bookings on cruise ships had dropped so much — and the great thing is they actually need our business, so it's not too likely they'll leave without us, babe.'

He gave a half-hearted grin at her little attempt at a joke.

Deborah leaned across to Connie, sitting on the other side of the aisle. 'Do you know if this cruise is fully booked?'

'Doubt it,' the old man replied. He pulled a pristine handkerchief out of his pocket and wiped his nose before adding, 'I made my reservations more than a month ago, and there were still plenty of staterooms left then. You all bought your tickets after I did with no problem. I suspect they'll be lucky to be at half capacity. Which will be great. More room for us.'

While Deb and Connie nattered on about the bookings, David stared forward out the driver's window. The unfamiliar brightly hued buildings of south Florida gave way to an eye-smarting view of the Atlantic. The sunlight lay pale gold on the choppy grey-blue waters.

Suddenly, the ship came into view. For one transcendent moment, all thoughts of the shooting incident and the hearing were washed from his mind. Subconsciously, his body swayed forward as he took in the narrow rectangular slice of ship, all sun-kissed white and royal blue inlaid with thin swirls of gold, against the deep blue sky. Stacked rows of windows and privacy-screened balconies dotted an expanse of smooth white hull, extending downward past the dock just visible in the foreground. Nearer the waterline, a row of bright orange lifeboats hung like toys by their davits. The shuttle moved closer, bringing the top deck of the ship and its spidery tracery of satellite arrays into clear view. Even from this distance, the *Nerissa* was massive, leviathan even, yet strangely elegant in its proportions. She looked like a beautiful woman, David thought, dressed up in her finest.

He sat transformed and strangely mute; for how long, he didn't know. Beautiful. Such an insignificant word . . .

Chip let out a low whistle. 'That's one big ship.'

'I'd hate to see how you boys would react if you saw one of those truly huge super-cruisers,' Connie said.

The shuttle suddenly shuddered to a stop. Everyone grabbed their bags and shuffled down the aisle en masse. They moved off the shuttle and onto the dock, where passengers from all the other shuttles were still gathered. Deb had been right, of course. They were nowhere near finished loading.

'We haven't missed a thing, I guess,' chirped Doreen. 'Looks like they're still loading all the old geezers.'

Chip shrugged and smiled at them,

visually apologetic for Doreen's crudeness.

Connie chortled at David's side. 'I guess she thinks it's charming to say stupid things.'

★　★　★

'Please, allow me to carry your bags into your room for you, Mrs. O'Conner.' The Third Purser gently lifted a carry-on from the frail-appearing elderly woman with the slightly vacant pink-tipped smile.

Mr. O'Conner beamed at the Purser in gratitude, saying as he held one thickly veined and mottled hand out for support, 'Mighty kind of you, son. Mildred and I appreciate it.'

Nearby onlookers smiled indulgently at the purser's thoughtfulness. Most of the Hermes Deck passengers were middle-aged, but the O'Conners were obviously very old and frail.

Morgance softly closed the door behind them and ran to the king-sized bed. Simultaneously yanking off her old-man wig and kicking off the heavy oxfords, she teased in Norman's wheeze, 'Now Mildred, dear, do be sure to give this nice young man a b-i-i-i-g tip, hear?'

Nevin glared at her as he pulled off his own wig and ran his fingers through his sweaty dark hair before sinking down on the bed and flopping over on his back.

Kostya stared down at them impassively. He reached into a pocket and extracted a bundle of neatly folded papers. 'Plans for the ship,' he explained. He laid the packet down next to Nevin, who had started to peel off Mildred's appliances. 'Everything's labeled, including the location of your other unregistered cabin on Pontus Deck. Whatever you need to know that isn't in there, I'll explain later.'

Morgance unbuttoned Norman's shirt, which covered the thick-ribbed white undershirt and bodysuit beneath it.

'Here's a couple of phony canceled tickets for the Pontus Deck couple, just in case you're asked for them,' Kostya continued. 'Your names are Neal and Melissa Hubèrt, and you're Canadian, which should make it easy for you. I'll be in touch later on, but right now I'm expected topside. More passengers are boarding.'

Morgance stepped out of her trousers. 'Is the cruise fully booked?'

'We're about at half capacity, give or take.'

'*Merci*. Bye,' she called after him, as he hurried out the door.

As the echo of his footsteps down the hall faded away, Morgance unfastened the Velcro tabs which held her body suit in place, and Nevin pulled away the last of his appliances as well, though none too gently.

'*Nevin, s'il vous plait!* Keep in mind we're going to have to reuse these things!'

Nevin placed the disembodied face of Mildred O'Conner carefully on the nightstand and slowly wiggled out of the glove-like hand appliances. In spite of his care, one tore along the juncture of the left thumb and palm-line. 'Sorry,' he said to her. 'I thought you were going to make extras.'

Speaking slowly so as not to lose her temper, she said evenly, 'Yes, I *did* make spares. But I'm not sure how many times we're going to need to use them, or how often we'll need to change back and forth each day. Just keep in mind that they can't be stretched. My formula's more delicate than latex. If it loses its elasticity, we'll need to use stronger adhesives, which take hours to apply and at least half an hour to remove. So *be careful!* OK, *mon cher?*'

Leaving the flayed faces and shucked-off hands of the O'Conners on the bed, like the shed carcasses of giant insects, they slipped into the cheaper set of tourist garments Kostya had left for them in the stateroom. Their new outfits were pathetically gauche but, as they donned the identities of the Canadian Hubèrts, Nevin and Morgance were well aware that blending in with the decidedly economy-class passengers of Pontus Deck was a must at this point in the plan.

★　★　★

Blake's X-ray showing the metal implants in his ravaged body allowed him to ignore the security scanner as he and Amyas boarded the ship, tickets and cabin assignments in hand.

Kenway's words continued to ring in his ears. *Remember — apart, we are but many . . .*

Kenway also had stressed that everyone involved in the enterprise should act as much like eager, happy tourists as possible, seeking out new friends and new opportunities. So Blake concentrated on smiling genially at his fellow passengers as he and Amyas worked their way through the thin line of people waiting for elevators to take them down to the economy Triton and Pontus Decks. A few of the women blushed when they noticed his attentions, and he nodded at them pleasantly.

He noticed that Amyas didn't seem to be having any difficulty blending in either. She flirted quite openly with some of the younger men. She was gorgeous, he had to admit. With her dark Columbian good looks, it was inevitable that men would notice her. But damn, did she have to be so obvious about it?

He had bent to whisper an admonition

in her ear when he noticed a man staring intently at him from about ten feet away. He was of slender build, but muscular, as if he worked out a lot. The woman standing next to him — his wife, probably — was pleasantly attractive but not beautiful. Then, to Blake's horror, a man standing next to the first guy also turned to gaze at Blake with inquisitive eyes. The two of them threw off a vibe Blake definitely didn't want to analyze. One thing was certain: both men were focused on him, not Amyas, which made him very uncomfortable.

They can't see my gun, Blake reasoned, so he smiled shyly and ventured out loud, 'Long wait, isn't it?' before putting his arm around Amyas and gently steering her closer to the elevators — and away from the still-staring strangers.

★   ★   ★

'What's up, Dave?'

Deb watched as the tall, handsome man with the petite, darkly beautiful woman drifted away from where they stood waiting for an elevator to their deck. The man had spoken to David and Carl, but the two cops had said nothing in return; and both continued to stare after the departing figures.

'That does *not* make any sense,' David said.

'What doesn't make sense?' Chip had moved up behind them.

'That rich guy — the one with the looker.' David nodded discretely in their direction.

'Oh, yeah. I see what ya mean.' Chip paused to scratch his ear before adding, 'Richie Rich with his little *peóna*. Looks like someone did their shopping in the red-light district maybe. All she needs is a price tag around her neck.'

'Or a bar code tattooed on her tush,' Carl agreed.

'No, that's not it,' Dave said. 'Just look at the guy. He's obviously wealthy. I mean look at the way his hair's cut; his *skin*, even. He looks like he just stepped out of an ad in the *Times*. Good-looking, fancy watch, diamond signet ring. So what's he doing dressed in cheap clothing in economy class with the rest of us working slobs?'

'Yeah, I guess you're right.' Carl nodded pensively. 'You'd expect him to be escorted in style to a deluxe stateroom on one of the upper decks like the one Connie booked, not standing here carrying his own bags and waiting for the down elevator.'

'Yeah, well if you think *that's* strange,' Chip said, pointing directly at a tall, ponytailed man of obvious Native American ethnicity, 'look at what *is* headed for the pricey deck.'

'Don't you recognize him?' Carl interrupted. 'He's been all over TV — *The Tonight Show*, everywhere.'

Chip looked blank.

'That's Richard Black Wolf,' Carl continued. 'He's an anthropologist, and he writes bestselling books. You must have seen him on TV. The guy's really famous — or infamous, depending on how you look at it.'

David grimaced. Thankfully, Black Wolf, or whatever his name was, took no notice of what those two idiots were saying about him. He watched the Indian activist out of the corner of his eye. The man seemed to care only about the taped box he was carrying. Dave hoped it wasn't animal parts, or cremains — or a bomb, even. Anything was possible these days, and the man's stoic expression hinted that his reason for sailing on the *Nerissa* probably had nothing to do with fine dining or the myriad entertainment possibilities. He tuned out Chip and Carl, who were still bantering away about their fellow passengers, but he kept an eye on the Indian, not so much out of curiosity, but because there was something about him that warranted further study.

He reflected that Richard Black Wolf was the first person he'd seen on board this ship of fools, aside from that nervous-looking young rich guy, who seemed to be as deep-down miserable as David found himself to be that afternoon.

★　★　★

'Finally . . . the Pontus Deck!'

David sat his carry-on down in the hall

gratefully, shoulders and upper-arm muscles aching from hauling their bags around. He and Deb were still trying to figure out fore from aft, let alone starboard from port, on the little deck map they'd been handed when they boarded. The cabins were numbered erratically and it was nearly impossible to find their quarters on their own. And, of course, there had been no purser in sight, despite the claim made for a high staff-to-passenger ratio as advertised in the brochure. As a result, there had been a very long wait for a crewman to direct them to their room.

Deb rooted around in her purse for the room key, prompting David to say in a voice that sounded ragged and mean, even to his own ears, 'I *know* you put 'em in there. Just dump the damn thing out on the floor.'

Deb's eyes flashed then glittered. As soon as he'd uttered the last word he could have kicked himself. 'Sorry, Deb. It's been a long day. Never mind me and my stupid remarks, OK?'

Blinking back the tears, she attempted a smile. 'Yeah, I've got a splitting headache myself. Ah! Here they are.' With a jangle of plastic and metal, she jammed the gold-plated key into the lock and turned it successfully.

Inside they found cool but stale air-conditioned darkness. Deb rushed ahead of him, hitching up her skirt as she made a beeline for the bathroom, slamming the hollow-core door behind her.

David started in after her, then turned to watch another couple enter a room a few doors down the corridor. He noted that they were carrying no bags at all, so he paused to get a better look at their faces.

Funny . . . he didn't recall seeing them earlier, either on any of the shuttles, or in the security-check line as they came aboard. He would have noticed them, he thought. The man was quite short and thin, albeit with a wiry build that warned he could probably hold his own in a bar fight or worse. His eyes were intensely bright and seemed confrontational when he glanced at Dave. *I'd hate to be around if this guy was pissed off*, he thought.

And the woman — she would have

caught his eye immediately, he thought. She was well-built and a bit taller than her companion. She wasn't exactly pretty, but her eyes were unusual — long-lashed, and slightly cat's-eye-shaped at the corners.

One other thing the street-savvy cop noticed: they were decidedly lower-class in their dress; pure K-Mart, just like that rich guy.

'What's wrong?' Deborah had emerged from the bathroom and came back out to pick one of her bags up off the carpet.

'Did you notice that couple down the hall?' he said, bringing in the rest of the bags. 'Short; around our ages, I'd guess. Well, I don't remember seeing them actually board the ship. What's more, they don't have any luggage. That's very odd, don't you think?'

'Babe . . . ' Her voice was weary. 'If I promise not to be a nurse on this cruise, then you must promise you'll stop being a cop long enough to enjoy the trip. OK?'

'Yeah, I promise,' he mumbled, even as he continued to eye the closed doorway down the hall with suspicion.

***

'Did you notice that idiot giving us the eye?' Morgance had that little edge in her voice that should have warned Nevin, but he was too engrossed in inspecting the room to pay her much heed.

True to their employers' word, Kostya had stowed everything else they needed in this extra stateroom: clothing for the Hubèrts, plus all the contingency items, including weapons, that they had discussed in the motel room on shore. The only thing missing, Nevin realized, was the requisite software codes. Apparently Kostya was to hold on to that particular piece of the puzzle until the exact moment it was needed for input.

Morgance gave an exasperated sigh, then looked around the cheap utility cabin which, according to Kostya, was not even on the registered list. They didn't exist as passengers, so long as they were holed up in here.

She rubbed her hands up and down the length of the Makarov revolver Kostya had left for her, smiling as her fingers caressed the cool, smooth metal; then she rubbed the bullets, each one, like beads on a rosary. Their employers had definitely come through for them, in style. The Makarov even had a silencer.

Nevin went to the porthole and pulled back the drape. 'Morgance!' he exclaimed to her over his shoulder. 'Come look! We're very close to the waterline here. It's perfect.'

★ ★ ★

'Did you see that fellow looking at us in the Purser's Square — the one who was about your height?'

Amyas sat on the edge of the cabin's one couch, bobbing a portable heat coil around in her mug of yerba mate. When the water was not quite boiling, she took out the heat coil and laid it on the slick laminated surface of the coffee table.

The sharp tang of burning wood made Blake drop the crisp shirts he was putting in the dresser and hurry to the electrical outlet, where he yanked out the infuser. 'Amyas! You could've started a fire! See

— the table's burned already!'

Amyas swirled out her *bombilla* in the mug of pungent yerba mate, smiling as she breathed in the herbal-scented steam. When she was done she looked up at him and teased, 'So? We won't be staying in this room for all that long, now, will we?'

Blake couldn't help but smile back at her. He couldn't resist her, nor could he maintain his anger when she blinked those eyes at him — eyes that could all but swallow his soul.

'No. I suppose not. But until then, we'll have to make do with this hovel. Now, could I possibly have a sip of that?'

'Here, try this.' Amyas took a deep sip of the herbal tea, then held it in her mouth while motioning for Blake to sit down beside her.

And when he wrapped his arms around her and their lips met, she very slowly let her tongue meet his, as the heady taste of yerba mate filled both their mouths, before she slid backwards on the cushion and Blake lowered himself down.

Once all of this is in motion for keeps, he told himself, *and we're far away from this ship, then things will be perfect between us.*

By his own calculations, only several hundred sea miles remained before the achievement of their most profound desire — and that of the Foundation, of course.

5

On the Zeus Deck, Richard Black Wolf had forced himself to wait before opening the box from Janice. First he unpacked the suitcase the purser had carried up to his stateroom, then shucked off his boots and shirt, and poured a club soda over ice from the mini-bar. Then, setting his glass on the coffee table in front of the couch, he began to tear away the layers of strapping tape.

Whatever was in the box didn't rattle; and knowing Janice as well as he did, Richard was sure that she had cocooned the object with layer upon layer of bubble-wrap and further wrapped it with sheets of newspaper from back home, so he could read the latest stories just as if they were curled up together on a Sunday morning, trading sections before working the crossword puzzle.

Ripping off the top of the box, he saw that he was correct about the newspaper.

Nothing like a tacit 'remember' subtext to bring home the sting of their separation.

There was a card on top, his first name written on the envelope in Janice's forward-slanting script. Not feeling quite up to reading it yet, mainly because he wouldn't have the luxury of the last word with her, Richard nursed his soda until he felt the ship begin to rumble beneath him.

Lurching forward imperceptibly, he heard the steam whistles on the surrounding tugboats blow, their keening shrill drone exceptionally loud in his top-of-the-ship suite. Stepping out onto the balcony, he was just in time to witness the *Nerissa* begin its graceful departure from the dock amid the throaty blare of tug-boat horns and cars honking from shore.

Relatively few tugs actually accompanied the ship: only four, and Richard guessed even these were mainly for show. But they, too, were beautiful in their own stubby, economical way — bright red-and-white-painted hulls, like children's toys shining in the sun-flecked blue-grey waters, each of them leaving a churned white wake aft as they guided the *Nerissa* into the Atlantic.

The air was briny but exhilarating, the breezes stiff but still soft against Richard's cheek. And as he gripped the balcony railing he thought, *God, Janice would've loved this. Hell, she should be here, not me. Damned if I can figure out what the hell happened.*

He stayed on the balcony until the last of the tugs headed back to Port Everglades. Behind him on the coffee table, the unopened card and gift waited, accusatorial in their silence.

Telling himself that the sun getting in his eyes was making them watery, Richard went back into the stateroom and sat down on the sofa and slid one thumb under the flap of the envelope.

The card inside had Chinese characters on the front and a few lines of handwriting within:

'Richard,
    You know I'd prefer to say this to your face. I am sorry about what I said,

of course. But more so about what happened. You didn't deserve this — but neither did I. And what's done is done.

I wish you all the best for this trip. Since Whiskers can't go with you, I thought this little fellow could serve double duty — conveying my hope that things will be better for you, and taking the spiritual place of our boy (who, by the way, isn't the only one who misses you!).

I suppose you can put this outside the door to guard you, or perhaps you can find a suitable altar for him in that fancy stateroom of yours.

Remember: despite what happened, a part of me will always love you.

Janice'

Richard's face showed no emotion as he put the card back into its envelope, but his fingers were trembling as he slid the newspaper-wrapped object out of the box and began to pull away the layers of packing until the ceramic sculpture within was revealed.

It was one of those Oriental good-luck cats for protection against the evil spirits. They were sold just about everywhere in San Francisco's Chinatown. She had chosen a white cat with rings of concentric yellow, tan and black dotting its paws and the top of its red-eared head. A red-and-gold collar adorned with a golden bell surmounted a gold-flecked green patch over its chest. It held a large gold-and-black medallion in its right paw, and the other paw was raised in greeting. A green paper tag with Chinese lettering was glued over its heart.

Richard could see something of his living cat in this ceramic substitute. The expression on its face was similar, as were its chubby contours. Yes, he could find a suitable shrine for this faux Whiskers.

He noticed a fine dusting of dark grey ash clinging to the head and paws of the likeness, and brushed some of it away reverently with one thumb. He had seen holy ash before and knew what it meant. Janice had chosen this gift to let him know that whatever had happened between them, there was no reason to blame their mutually owned cat. No matter what else she might claim to feel or think about him, Richard knew that the cat was exempt from all the bitterness that sprang out of their quarrels.

Placing the porcelain cat on the nightstand near his bed, Richard reflected on this voyage into unknown parts. *I bet I'm not the only one who's going to need some luck on this damn ship*, he predicted.

He rubbed the head of the silent yellow-eyed cat and closed his own eyes. He placed one finger over his lips, lest the sound of his sobbing echo too loudly in his own ears.

★   ★   ★

It was still early when David awoke the next morning, slightly disoriented and groggy from a somewhat sleepless night. He quietly moved to the bathroom and took care of his morning ablutions, then examined his suitcase. Deb had shopped and packed for both of them, and she had thoughtfully packaged a set of underwear, socks, shirt and matching slacks in separate packets. He didn't have to think about it at all, just grab the first packet and dress quickly, and without much regard to style.

He peeked at the still-sleeping Deborah once more, then tiptoed to the door and stepped out into the hall. All quiet out here as well. He guessed that most of the others were either sea-sick or hungover this morning, with the possible exception of Connie, who knew how to nurse a drink. He decided to head to the upper deck, take a quick walk around to get the lay of the ship, then find some breakfast.

As he strolled along the deck, sniffing the salt air and glancing from time to time out at the white caps sparkling in the early-morning sun, he reviewed in his mind again the disparities he had noted at boarding.

That elderly couple. There was definitely something amiss there; more than just advanced age and physical handicaps would allow for. He couldn't quite put his finger on it, but his cop's instinct told him they were hiding something. What could it be? They seemed fairly ordinary; a well-off old couple enjoying a well-deserved vacation in the sun. But there was something in the way they moved, acted, spoke, and the way they played off each other that seemed out of place.

What was it the man had said? 'Did you remember to wear the right shoes?' What a strange thing for a man to say to his wife. And her response: 'I think so. Do these look all right?' while sticking out a foot and pulling up her pants leg just a smidge. That just seemed . . . odd.

They didn't realize, of course, that David was hovering near and had overheard this brief exchange. He was accustomed to operating like a fly on the wall. It came naturally to him after all these years, and he probably wasn't going to stop now. Some people would say it was eavesdropping or snooping, but he didn't see it that way. It was just an extension of who he was, and he couldn't change now if he wanted to. And sometimes it came in handy.

He glanced up and paused. A sign over a deckside entrance read: 'Exercise Room:

Weight Machines and Spa. Instructions Available.' After a moment of hesitation, David entered the brightly lit facility. He approached the desk, where a young man dressed in shorts and a body shirt sat engrossed in the computer station in front of him.

'Hello, may I help you?' the assistant asked as Dave glanced through a few brochures.

'Just looking around. I might be interested in coming in later on and doing a few sets. What hours are you open, and do I need to register or anything?'

'Nope. We're open from six a.m. until midnight, so you're welcome to stop in anytime. Are you familiar with the machines? We'll be happy to provide instruction.'

'No, I work out pretty regularly, and these all look like the standard equipment I'm familiar with.' Dave gestured at the various fixtures scattered about the room. A few serious body-builders were grunting and groaning at one or two stations in the back, but other than that, the room was quiet.

'Fine. Let me give you a few of these

brochures; and please, come on in any time you'd like. Happy to have you aboard!'

'Thanks.' Dave took a plastic bag stuffed with flyers and brochures from the young man. He started to turn away, then stopped. 'Is there any place I could grab breakfast nearby? That's really what I started out looking for this morning.'

'Oh, sure. Right over there.' The young man gestured at double doors off to one side. 'That's our lounge, and I'm sure they're serving breakfast in there now. Go check it out.'

'I will. Thanks. Sounds great.'

Dave crossed the room and entered the lounge. It was nearly empty, but looked bright and cheerful. He could hear a clattering of pots and pans coming from the kitchen area, and the smell of coffee and frying bacon permeated the air.

He headed toward an empty booth near the back of the room, then stopped at the sound of a man's voice. 'Good morning! We seem to be the only ones up and about this morning. Care to join me?'

It was the anthropologist, Richard

Black Wolf. Dave didn't know how to respond. He really would rather be by himself, but he didn't want to offend the man.

'I think most of my buddies partied too hearty last evening,' he said finally, stopping at Richard's table. 'Are you sure you want company? I don't want to impose.'

'Nonsense. I could use a little companionship — and you look like you could, too. Join me, please?'

'All right.' Dave sat down in the offered chair. 'David Spaulding,' he added, in way of introduction.

'Richard Black Wolf.' Richard rose slightly and offered his hand. 'Good to meet you. I realize you're with a party, but since you wandered in here alone, I just assumed you're the early riser in your group — like me.' He smiled.

'I do like to get going early in the morning. I didn't sleep very well last night — strange bed and all the excitement. So when I woke up this morning I just decided to get up and get going. I don't think the rest of my gang will be up and about for a while yet.' He grinned. 'Those who aren't sea-sick are probably hung-over.'

'Got it.' Richard smiled back. 'I try to take it easy on the booze . . . my heritage and all that. Us Injuns have enough trouble taming our demons; no point in adding firewater to the mix!'

Dave laughed. 'I'm a bit cautious myself. I'm a police officer by profession, and I try to stay on the straight and narrow as well. Just like your people, mine have a tendency to go down the wrong path from time to time. Pressure of the job, y'know.'

'It's a good practice,' Richard acknow-ledged. 'I try to be the first to arrive at a party and the first to leave. Hasn't failed me yet. By the way, don't let me step out of bounds, but I sense we're kindred spirits. Being with the police, I suspect you're an observer of the people around you. Has anything struck you as odd — since we boarded, I mean? You don't have to answer that, of course, but a few things have been bothering me. You look like a level-headed guy. I'd just like to get your take on it; see if you've noticed a few of the things I have.'

'Now that you mention it,' Dave said, 'I *have* noticed one or two things about some of our fellow passengers that don't seem to jibe.' He paused. He didn't ordinarily talk this openly to anyone, let alone a relative stranger. Somehow it felt right, though, and he continued his train of thought. 'Some of these so-called passengers just don't seem to fit the mold of what makes sense to me. I've heard a few conversations that have been down-right puzzling. I really don't know what to make of it.'

They paused as the waiter came up to take their orders and fill their cups with steaming-hot coffee. Richard added cream and sugar to his mug and took an appreciative sip. 'The thing with loners — I recognize a fellow 'lone wolf' when I see him — is we tend to stay in the background, stay quiet, and listen carefully to what is said around us. Am I right about that?'

'The Black Wolf is a 'lone wolf,' eh?' Dave smiled. 'Yes, I think you could call me a lone wolf. I tend to stick to myself by preference. Sitting here having breakfast with you, a relative stranger, is completely out of character for me. But I have to say I'm enjoying it — enjoying your company. So I think we *are* fellow lone wolves; outriders in the pack.'

'Good take on it, Dave. I couldn't have said it better myself, and they gave me a piece of paper a while back that says I know what I'm talking about. But to get back to what I was saying; let me throw a few observations out there and see if they resonate with you. The elderly couple — the O'Conners, I think is their name — anything strike you odd about them?'

'Funny you should mention them. I was just thinking about them this morning. They had a very strange conversation when they didn't think I was close enough to hear them, or maybe they thought I wasn't paying attention. Something about, was the wife wearing the right kind of shoes. Maybe she's getting Alzheimer's and was just reassuring herself, but it sounded pretty weird to me.'

'Right. And *I* heard them talking about 'the other cabin,' as if they had a double booking or something. That's more than strange. What would a little old couple be doing with *two* cabins on an ocean cruise that may very well have put a pretty big dent in their life savings? Weird, I'll say.'

'Hmm. Okay, that's the old couple. How about the young rich guy? Harvard or Yale type, with lots of Daddy's money to spread around. Why in the world is he down below decks in a cramped steerage accommodation? Now that *really* doesn't make any sense. Why would he even bother taking a luxury cruise, without the luxury? And did you notice that voluptuous Latin beauty keeping an eye on him? It was almost as if she was his mother spying on him to make sure he didn't get into trouble.'

'Ah yes, the young Mr. Bainbridge. Well, you see, I happen to have met his father at some point. I don't know if he's aware of that fact or not, but I got the distinct impression he was trying to avoid me. And Ms. Copacabana gave off all the vibes of a watchdog, not a girlfriend.'

'You know his father? What's the scoop? Any back story on this guy?'

'Not really. I only met him as part of a promotional tour I was making on behalf of my last book. I often get introduced to VIPs casually, especially if they've bought in to a 'meet and greet the author' kind of event. I think that was how I met Bainbridge, Sr. We only chatted for a few minutes, and I don't recall he said anything about his son; just ordinary conversation. But it just strikes me as odd, like you said, that the kid would be on his own here, in bad accommodation and apparently under the watchful eye of a nanny-type caretaker, lovely as she is.'

Their meals arrived and the next few minutes were spent in buttering toast, ordering more coffee and tucking into heaping plates of bacon, eggs and home fries. Finally Richard sat back, wiped his face with a snow-white napkin, and continued the conversation. 'Anyone else seem out of place amongst the usual suspects?'

'Now that you mention it, how about that 30-something couple with the cheap get-ups? They acted like fish out of water, although I could see them in economy class.'

'Yeah. I noticed how the guy kept rubbing his face, almost as if he had something stuck on there and was trying to get rid of it.'

'If I didn't know better,' Dave interposed, 'I could almost think he might have been wearing some sort of facial disguise recently. I've seen guys who have tried to disguise themselves to get out of an arrest; they act exactly the same way.'

'They have some sort of accent I couldn't quite place,' added Richard. 'Just a tone or inflection, almost like what you hear in Minnesota. Know what I mean?'

'Yeah.' Dave scratched his head and shoved his nearly empty plate back. 'How about Canadian? Does that ring a bell?'

'I think you could be right about that.' Richard grabbed for the check when the waiter brought it around, added his room number and signed with a flourish. As Dave protested, he waved his hand. 'Naw. Don't think anything about it. My expenses on this trip are being paid by my publisher, thanks to my ever-vigilant agent. You can get the next meal, if you'd like.' He glanced at Dave in a questioning manner.

'Sure, I'd be glad to do that. I've enjoyed our talk this morning. Given us both something to think about, that's for sure. If you have no objection, I'd like to continue the conversation later on. I have to meet my fiancée for lunch, but perhaps you'd like to join us for dinner? I'd like her to meet you.'

Richard took out a business card and wrote his room number on the back. 'Just call later on and let me know time and place. I'm going to be working in my room most of the afternoon, so I'll be ready for a good meal.'

Dave stood up, reached over and shook Richard's hand. The two men smiled at each other. It had been an enlightening morning after all, and Dave left the exercise area with a spring in his step. Perhaps this cruise would be more interesting than he expected.

He entered their darkened room quietly so as not to disturb Deb should she still be sleeping. He needn't have bothered. The bed was freshly made up and he grabbed the folded paper under the foil-wrapped chocolate on his pillow.

Hi:
I'm meeting the girls at the chapel to nail down the ceremony plans. Am I correct that you don't need to weigh in on flowers, etc.? Figure you'll be out and about exploring everything and can fill me in on your adventures later. Shall we meet for drinks and tapas mid-afternoon? Just text me (or I'll text you when I'm finished with all this planning stuff). Have a good morning.

Love,
Deb

She was right about that. He didn't need to be consulted about the flowers and such. All that was important to her, and he wanted her to have her day with everything perfect, but it didn't mean a hill of beans to him.

He opened the room-darkening drapes

and the sliding doors out to their tiny balcony. He stepped out for a moment, then resolutely turned back into the room and took a seat at the desk. Pulling a pad of paper towards him, he took out a pen and began jotting down notes about the anomalies he and Richard had observed and overheard the day before.

After a bit he stood and stretched, popped the chocolate into his mouth and retrieved a soda from the room fridge. But his mind was still working, spinning scenarios and possible connections between the passengers in question.

One thing he realized: he was feeling a lot more positive about his situation than he had in quite a while. He wouldn't go so far as to say he was back to normal yet — that was going to require hard work on his part. But he felt good, using his brain again for the first time in a long time.

And he had enjoyed his conversation with his new friend this morning. The guy seemed to really have his head screwed on right. He had felt very comfortable discussing what were probably just silly conspiracy theories. Still, it gave him a lot more confidence to realize that someone else — someone whose opinion he *respected* — seemed to see things the same way he did.

Refreshed, he sat back down and, with renewed vigor, again put pen to paper, sketching out possible connections and motives for his shipboard companions' strange ways.

By the time he had taken a quick shower and changed for dinner, Deb had texted him with directions to a bar/restaurant near the chapel area on one of the upper decks. He responded, asking if she minded if he invited someone else to join them. She responded with a quick 'Sure,' but he could intuit her surprise. He called Richard's room and was just about to hang up when the other man picked up.

'Yes?' Richard's voice seemed a bit rough, as if he had been coughing.

'Hi. It's David Spaulding. We shared breakfast earlier. My fiancée and I are meeting for drinks and dinner at the Marina Bar on the Chapel Deck. Would you care to join us? I'd like to introduce you to her and repay your hospitality this morning.'

'Oh, yes. Sorry. I've been working on my book most of the afternoon. Putting notes together and trying to put together the outline. I'm ready for a break. Sounds great. Shall I meet you there in about twenty minutes?'

'Fine. Looking forward to it.' So Richard had been doing about the same thing he had today. Funny, how a perfect stranger could seem so compatible so quickly. He wondered if Richard had given any more thought to their morning discussions. It would be interesting to see if he had come up with any of the same possibilities.

He glanced about the room, hesitated, then folded over the several pages he had covered with notes and stuffed them in his back pocket. He'd wait and see if the topic came up, but you never knew.

★ ★ ★

Nevin stood a long time, looking out over the dark blue waters tinged with lacy white foam. He shivered a bit and pulled the knitted shawl about his shoulders. Then he clomped a bit ungracefully back inside and glanced at Morgance, just putting the last bit of padding into her slacks before donning a pristine dinner jacket laid out on the bed.

'You just about ready?' he asked, swishing his tongue over his front teeth to remove any errant bit of lip gloss.

'Eh?' she asked, pulling the jacket on and taking a quick glance in the mirror. Subconsciously she patted the wig that covered her normally glossy hair. He had noticed the habit and had spoken rather sharply to her about it earlier. 'You need to act more like a man, not a woman,' he had said, looking about quickly in the dim corridor. He thought that famous author, standing a little further down, was too far away to hear him. The man didn't react so he felt safe.

'Stop picking at me,' Morgance had responded in her natural voice with the slight Canadian accent. 'I'll act how I want to act. Don't be such a nit-picker.'

The incident had passed quickly, but

still he felt a little uncertain, as if this whole masquerade was becoming more than the two of them were capable of pulling off. For one thing, he was having difficulty in remembering just which part he was playing — and why. When they made an appearance as the elderly couple, he had to stop and think what he was doing, and not revert back into their more natural roles as their younger selves. *With the too-cheap clothing*, he reminded himself. *That was really a stupid mistake on the part of the Russians.* And one that might very well come back to haunt them.

'All right, then,' he grumped in his naturally gruff voice, seeming very odd indeed coming from the pink lips of the little old lady. 'Let's get this show on the road.'

* * *

'But how could they possibly connect?' Richard Black Wolf sipped his soda and sighed. 'I just don't get it.'

'Maybe they're not connected at all,'

Dave replied. 'After all, a cruise ship as large as this one is sort of like a small town. Any place large enough to have this many people concentrated in it is a mecca for all sorts, including petty thieves — and worse.'

Deb had not said much as the two men continued their conversation, but she had been thinking hard and now she spoke up. 'What if there are several different things going on? More than one criminal conspiracy, for instance, and they just happened to coincide at this particular time in this particular place? Isn't that the most likely possibility?'

'Occam's razor,' said Richard. 'Of course. Here we've been trying to come up with all sorts of complicated schemes and scenarios. But what if it's as simple as more than one crook, or group of crooks, serendipitously coming aboard at the same time? I mean after all, you could make up an elaborate plan, fine-tune it and everything, then be flummoxed when SOD — Some Other Dude — comes in and steals your thunder.'

'I think you've got something there,

Deb,' Dave said, smiling at her. 'I think you might just have hit the nail on the head. I think we're dealing with several different shady types. They just *happen* to be here together; doesn't mean they're working together at all.'

'Whoa!' Deb put up her hands in mock horror. 'What are you saying, 'We're dealing with' this situation? I don't think it's our issue at all. Go to the captain or someone with your theories, guys, but please, leave the sleuthing to someone else. We've got a wedding to plan!'

'Sure,' Dave said. 'Of course you're right. I've certainly got no power here at all, and if there really is something nefarious going on, the authorities need to know about it.'

'And do you think they'll take what we tell them seriously?' put in Richard. 'I mean, what do we have, anyway? Just a few words overheard here and there; an anomaly or two, or three. We have no proof that any of these people have done anything wrong, nor do we know for sure they're planning anything. I don't know about you, Dave, but I'm inclined to keep my opinions to myself and watch and wait. If there *is* something going on, we should be able to spot it before it gets out of hand. Then we can offer our theory to the captain. I think they'll just laugh at us otherwise.'

'You're probably right about that,' said Dave. 'Why don't we wait a day or two and keep an eye on these people. If we see or hear anything more concrete, we can go to the authorities together and make a cohesive report.'

'Sounds like a plan to me,' Richard agreed. 'Now, I think I see our waiter signaling us to our table. I don't know about you, but all this brain work has made me hungry!'

'Me, too,' laughed Deb, and Dave ushered her to their table. 'By the way, Mr. Black Wolf, you know you're invited to our wedding, don't you? And no gifts required. Seeing Dave this interested and engaged again is more than enough of a gift for me.'

'Richard, please. And I'll be delighted to attend your wedding. I could stand with a happy occasion right about now.

But I'm just as glad to be 'interested and engaged' again as well. I sincerely hope we haven't uncovered something truly ugly here, but I do love a mystery, and I think we have one on our hands.'

David Spaulding walked with his beloved and his newfound friend across the bar and into the adjacent dining room. He thought about what both Deb and Richard had said and realized that he was suddenly looking forward to dinner, to his upcoming marriage, and to solving mysteries with a new friend.

6

'I think it's just a scam,' said Rachel, tossing her hair with a sniff. 'I never heard anything so crazy in all my life.'

'I don't, know Rach. It sounds sorta interesting to me.' Doreen examined a ragged fingernail and attacked it with her emery board.

Deborah sighed. The three of them were stretched out on the sunny side of the observation deck. The conversation had started out light, with enthusiasm all around for her planned wedding and celebration now scheduled for this evening, Christmas Eve. But at some point the other two began discussing the mysterious and exotic woman, Amyas, and her handsome boyfriend, Blake. The couple belonged to some cult organization known only as the Foundation, and apparently there were other members of their group aboard the *Nerissa* as well.

'Did they ask for any money? Donations

or anything?' Deborah smoothed some lotion on her legs and arms. The last thing she wanted to do was deal with a bad case of sunburn at her wedding.

'No . . . ' Doreen hesitated. 'Well, no, not really. There was some mention of 'shares' or something that you could purchase, just like any other business opportunity. Blake seems to have plenty of money, and that Amyas dresses like a million bucks.'

'I'd be really skeptical of that,' Rachel put in, turning over on her stomach. 'Hey, Deb, put some of that on my shoulders, would you? I don't want to look like a lobster tonight.'

'Why don't we go inside and get something cool to drink? I think I've had enough sun for a while.' Deb was a little irked. Doreen was so taken with this new rich couple that she seemed to have lost complete interest in the wedding and party afterward.

Rachel got up immediately, but Doreen hesitated. 'I think I'll just stay out here a little longer. Amyas said she might meet me here. I'd hate to miss her. You two go on. I'll catch up with you later.'

Deborah didn't say anything, but a quick wave of resentment brushed over her. This Amyas was stealing her thunder.

Come on, Rachel,' she said, ignoring Doreen. 'I'll buy you a drink. I think I could use one.'

★ ★ ★

But Amyas was occupied elsewhere. 'Get your head together!' she hissed.

Blake was standing on the other side of their balcony's protective railing, head down, teetering back and forth, and dangerously close to the edge.

Amyas took a deep breath and tried again. 'Come on, sweetie,' she said a little more gently. 'I'm right here and I'm not going to let you go. Come back in now and let's talk about it.'

Blake wavered a moment, then seemed to make up his mind. Slowly, gritting his teeth as he bent his bad leg, he crawled back over the railing and stood uncertainly in the doorway.

'I just feel so guilty,' he said. 'I've

betrayed my father. I'm so weak I can't even make a damned decision for myself. I'm a failure,' he moaned, tears streaming down his face. 'I'm nothing but a stupid failure.'

'Nonsense.' Amyas took his arm and guided him to the bed, where he sat down heavily, head in hands, and continued to rock back and forth, moaning softly. She went to the bathroom and brought back a glass of water and several pills. 'Here, take these. They'll calm you down. Then you can rest for a bit before we need to join the others.'

'No!' Blake shouted. 'No more dope! That's part of what's wrong with me; why I can't think straight.'

'It's not dope,' she insisted. 'These are very mild tranquilizers. You know the doctor said you needed something to help you relax. Please, Blake. Help me out here. You're not the only one who has issues, remember?'

He grabbed the glass and pills, shoved them in his mouth and gulped them down with the water. 'Fine. Are you satisfied? Now, let me try and get a little sleep before I need to get back into character again. I'll do my part, but you're going to have to do yours. Don't desert me, Amyas. I can't pull any of this off without you.' He lay back on the bed and closed his eyes. His head was still pounding, but the edge was off now, and everything was beginning to fade. Yes, this *was* better. At least he would be able to sleep for a bit.

Amyas closed the door to the balcony, locked it, and pulled the drapes closed. She adjusted the air conditioning, glanced at the still form on the bed, then left the room. She had a lot to accomplish in a very short time. She couldn't afford to let these tantrums of Blake's deter her.

She glanced at her watch. Darn! She had probably missed that stupid woman — what was her name? Dora? Doreen? Oh well, there were the others. That group from Milwaukee — they had all seemed interested, as had that dishy anthropologist with the crazy name, Black Wolf. He had talked to her quite a little while earlier, after overhearing her pitch to the ladies. He asked a lot of questions about the Foundation and its precepts.

All they would need would be someone like him — someone with celebrity — to spread the word about this wonderful new Cause. Yes, she would look up Richard Black Wolf; get him on board. Then they would all come . . . like sheep to the slaughter.

★   ★   ★

'Where the hell is she?' Chip's voice had an edge to it, like finely honed steel. He glanced over accusingly at Rachel. 'You're the last one to see her, Rach. Did she say where she was going?'

Rachel wiggled uncomfortably in her too-tight bridesmaid's gown. 'You know how she is, Chip. She's always got some bee in her bonnet.'

David tried not to show his exasperation. Here they were, just about to start the ceremony, and Doreen — Dumb Dora, as he and Connie had called her in private — was nowhere to be found. Everyone else was here, including some of the invited guests from among the passengers they had met on board. Captain Jones, accompanied by some of his officers, had made his appearance and had already gone over what would happen during the brief ceremony with David and Deb.

There was one other absentee, he suddenly realized. Richard Black Wolf was not there either. He wondered if the man was staying away deliberately to avoid stealing their thunder with his celebrity. Would be like him.

But right at this moment, a decision had to be made. Deb was keeping a stiff upper lip, but he could tell she was nervous and close to tears. 'All right,' he said loudly, 'I think we should just go ahead. She may have taken a nap and overslept. It's okay,' he added, turning to the fuming Chip. 'It's no big deal. She can join us for the reception.'

The others began moving toward the front of the intimate chapel, decorated for the occasion with flowers picked out especially by Deborah and her friends earlier. The cloying scent reminded David too much of a funeral, but he said nothing and took his place near the altar.

Captain Jones was already standing there, glancing at a small black book opened up on the lectern. Chip stood next to David, acting as best man, and Carl escorted the guests who were still milling around to their seats.

A hush hovered over the room and David looked expectantly at the door of the anteroom in the rear, expecting to see a beaming Deborah escorted by Connie come slowly down the narrow aisle.

Suddenly, the rear doors to the deck beyond burst open and Richard Black Wolf came running in and down the aisle.

'Something's happened!' he shouted. 'Please, everyone listen to me carefully. There has been an attempt to take over the ship, Captain.' He turned to the officer staring at him in shock. 'We need your advice and leadership right now. All able-bodied men — gather around while I explain what I've just witnessed.'

'Are you out of your mind?' thundered the captain. 'What in the world are you talking about? Take over the ship? That's impossible!'

'No, sir. Please hear me out and let me

explain. The Foundation cult members have compromised the rest of your officers and crew and have forced them to shut down the motors. I don't know what else they're planning, but it can't be good. Hurry, please! We're all in great danger, and we must move quickly if we are to save ourselves.'

★ ★ ★

Nevin had been trying to nap when a loud pounding at their cabin door roused him. 'Who . . . what is it?' he mumbled, dragging himself to his feet and heading toward the door.

Morgance, he could hear, was in the shower. They were about to dress up again as the O'Conners before joining the Spaulding wedding reception. Their whole deck had been invited, and he was not looking forward to it. He hoped they could put in a brief appearance and then leave early.

'It is I, Kostya! Something's happened! You must let me in!'

Nevin threw open the door. Kostya thrust himself through the open portal and fell into the nearest chair, where he sat panting, while Nevin eyed him with suspicion and apprehension.

'What's wrong, Kostya?' Nevin felt cold perspiration soaking the back of Mrs. O'Conner's silk blouse. 'What's going on?'

Just then the bathroom door opened and, in a cloud of perfumed steam, Morgance entered the room wearing one of the ship's luxurious terry robes, her freshly shampooed hair wrapped tightly in a towel. 'What are *you* doing here?' she said to Kostya in surprise. 'I thought you were keeping an eye on the officers' lounge.'

'It's terrible,' Kostya began, almost as if he were muttering to himself. 'It's all gone wrong! I don't know if we can salvage the operation or not.' He threw his head into his hands and began groaning and weaving back and forth in his seat.

'*What's gone wrong?*' Morgance shouted at him, grabbing his hands and pulling them from his face. 'Speak up, damn you! Tell us whatever you're gibbering about! *Now!*'

133

'It's that group — you know, the Foundation or whatever they call themselves.' Kostya actually had tears in his eyes as he spoke. 'They're out-maneuvering us. They're in the act, right now, of taking over the ship! They've not only shut down the engines, they've also been able to deploy the anchors to keep us from drifting.'

'*What?*' Nevin jumped to his feet and shoved Morgance out of the way as he hauled the blubbering Kostya to his feet. '*What in the hell do you mean, they're taking over the ship?* And how the hell can they drop the anchors? Aren't we at sea?'

Kostya pulled Nevin's hand off his arm and pulled himself upright. 'I *mean* just what I said. We're now close to the first port of call, and the waters here are shallow enough to deploy the anchors. And you, you little rat, *you keep your hands off me!*'

Morgance stepped between the two men and pulled Kostya to one side. 'He didn't mean anything, Kostya. We're just a . . . a little confused by all this. What do you think we should do now?'

'I don't see how we can continue under these circumstances. Any of the ship's officers who haven't been compromised will surely try to take back control, and that means we've lost the element of surprise we were counting on.' Kostya sat back down and Nevin, with a nod from Morgance, moved to the other side of the room.

'Hmm . . . I don't know.' Morgance had removed the towel from her hair and, turning toward the dressing table, began running a comb through the tangled tresses. 'You say the anchors are deployed. I wonder if somehow we might be able to make use of this situation. Where is it all taking place?'

'They're all up on the top deck, near the front of the ship. It looks as if there were more Foundation members aboard than we realized. I suppose some of them were traveling incognito. Plus they've now recruited a surprising number of the other passengers to their cause. They're going on and on, and that Kenway fellow is making speeches about this being their 'opportunity to make a new and better world for the future,' or some such nonsense. They seem to have their people in a hypnotic trance of some sort, and they're holding the ship's crew and some of the other passengers hostage below decks with weapons. I have no idea what their ultimate goal is, but I don't see how we can stop them.' He looked at them dourly.

Morgance jumped to her feet. 'Here's what we're going to do.' She rapidly put her plan to the others. Then: 'Kostya, you get back up on deck and do just as I explained. We've got to act right now if we're going to pull this thing off. Nevin,' she barked, 'get back in disguise. I'll have a couple of adjustments to make; then you'll have to give the strongest performance of your life if we are to succeed.'

She ran to the wardrobe and began pulling out clothing. 'Go, Kostya! Go now!' she yelled at him. 'And for God's sake, keep your wits about you!'

★   ★   ★

Captain Jones, with his several officers who had joined him in the chapel,

136

together with David and Richard, began organizing the men in their party and taking stock of what advantages they might have against Kenway and his followers.

'Here.' The captain gestured at a small printed diagram of the ship's layout in the flyers stacked on one of the tables. 'If we can get the women and older people down this passageway and onto one of the lower decks, they may be able to keep out of sight until we can secure the upper deck and the main control room.'

'Are there any weapons stashed anywhere we can lay our hands on?' David asked. He felt naked without his trusty revolver. He and the others had all left their weapons at home, given the supposedly peaceful nature of this trip. Now he wondered why he had let Connie talk him into going on this cruise in the first place. If it was to calm his nerves and get rid of his nightmares, well, it wasn't going to happen here!

'We have a couple of hand guns on us, and there are side-arms locked up in the control room,' answered the captain. 'But we'll have to get there first. Hopefully these idiots haven't beaten us to it. How the hell did *you* get away?' he added, turning to Richard. 'Didn't they see you?'

'I kept moving along the perimeter of the crowd; and when everyone's attention was turned toward the speaker, I simply popped behind a column, then back into one of those open service corridors. Nobody noticed me at all. Just the Indian in me, I guess.' He smiled ruefully. 'Us braves have our ways.'

'Well, we're all thankful to you for having the nerve to do it. No telling what they would have done had they stopped you.'

Connie edged forward and interrupted with a quavering voice. 'I demand to know what *you*, Captain, are going to do about this debacle. I'm not feeling so well, and I'm sure some of these ladies here are frightened and uncertain.' He wavered a bit, as if about to pass out, but caught himself, adding, 'You need to be taking steps to protect us, and I don't care what you have to do to keep us safe.'

For the first time since he had known

the man, David felt ashamed and more than just a bit angry at his mentor. The man sounded like a coward — the last thing one would expect of a highly decorated former police officer. He moved next to Connie and took hold of his elbow, neatly maneuvering him away from the officers and other men.

'What are you doing?' he mouthed. 'Can't you see we have a real emergency here? Whining about it isn't going to help. You need to go sit down and keep your mouth shut before you get everybody else upset too.' So saying, he gently but firmly steered Connie out of the close-knit group and sat him down in one of the rows of chairs set up for the ceremony — which was now postponed, perhaps indefinitely.

David glanced around for Deb, spotted her speaking earnestly in a corner to Rachel, and gave her a nod. She excused herself and hurried over to where David was standing next to the seated but quivering Connie.

'What's wrong?' she asked anxiously. He could see the trace of tears on her cheek but, like the trooper she was, she had pulled herself together and was eager to help if she could.

'Connie's feeling a bit under the weather. I think you'd better keep an eye on him, see if you can keep him comfortable. I think we're going to try and move the women and older people to a safer location. Soon, I hope. See what you can do for him, will you?' He gave her a quick kiss on the cheek.

'Sure, babe. I'll just sit down here with him and talk to him a bit. Maybe I'd better see if I can take his pulse. Make sure nothing else is going on.' She paused a moment before adding, 'I sure hope Doreen's okay. Rachel said she might actually have planned to attend this meeting or rally or whatever they were calling it. Do you think this is all just a big misunderstanding?'

'I don't know. Richard seemed to believe it was for real, and I trust his judgment. I don't know why they would stop the ship, and I can't for the life of me think what they hope to accomplish with this insane move.'

'Well, I don't want you to worry about me,' she said, brushing aside a tendril of hair and patting his hand. 'I'm strong and I can keep my wits about me. I'll look after Connie and Rachel and any of the others who need me. I know you have to do this.' She nodded toward the group of serious-faced men studying the ship's diagram. 'I'll be waiting for you,' she whispered, 'whenever this damn thing is resolved. And I know with you in the mix, it *will* be resolved. After all, we still have a wedding ahead of us.'

At that moment David understood, perhaps for the first time, just what it was to love someone unconditionally. He leaned over and kissed her again, this time on the mouth.

'Stay safe, Deb,' he whispered urgently. 'You stay safe and wait for me. I promise you, we'll come back here and do this. I swear it by all that's holy to me.'

★ ★ ★

Nevin twitched at the tweed skirt in exasperation.

'What are you *doing*?' hissed Morgance, grabbing at his hand and pulling it away from the fabric. 'We mustn't draw attention to ourselves until we're in place.'

She had gone over her plan with Kostya and Nevin, urging them to pay close attention to every detail. Everything hinged on split-second timing, and they still would need to count on the Foundation members being somewhat uncertain of themselves for everything to work.

Both men seemed to have lost all initiative, she thought in disgust. Leave it to the men to go all wimpy at the slightest hint of danger. At least she had *her* wits about her. She considered every possibility for error as she rushed with them through the rat's warren of back passageways. No. It *would* work. They just had to take every advantage of that thin edge of surprise. She smiled to herself as she thought how stunned they all would be if — *when* — she had pulled this off properly.

'*Here!*' She ground to a halt at the last doorway, which she knew from the diagrams they'd studied opened out onto the deck. It was used primarily by the stewards and servers and ship's personnel to deliver food and other items to passengers lounging about. She was certain most of those gathered outside the unobtrusive entry would be paying little or no attention to this area.

'Now, Kostya, you move into position just inside the deck area, but behind that column there.' She pointed. 'Nevin, you must go into your act. You know what you need to do. We can't waste any time at all on this. *Everything* relies on this one next part.'

Nevin, nervously touching the lace blouse edging at his neck, minced carefully out onto the promenade side of the deck and began inching his way toward a narrow viewing platform that stretched out over the side of the ship. The little gate was normally kept locked, and passengers could only access it with the permission and assistance of one of the ship's personnel, mainly for safety reasons. At the top of a steep, almost ladder-like incline of steps, the platform was quite small, but still large enough to accommodate a large telescope that was used for observing both the vista beyond and the occasional sea life below.

Morgance, disguised as Mr. O'Conner, trailed along behind, eyeing both Kostya, who had already reached the gate, and Nevin coming at it from another angle. Anxiously she scanned the sea of faces, now upturned rapturously as they took in the hypnotic intonations of Kenway Trumball. Then her eagle eye soon found the one face she sought — Blake Bainbridge. He looked nervous and sweaty, she thought. Good. She had already made the determination that the young man had some sort of psychological problem — and he appeared to her, at times, to be under the influence of some sort of narcotic. All the better. It would make her job easier.

She moved in swiftly, excusing herself as she brushed against those she passed, until she was suddenly standing right next to Bainbridge. She looked cautiously around. His constant companion, Amyas, was up at the front of the group, standing next to Kenway with a triumphant smile on her face, nodding and encouraging him as he spoke.

'Excuse me, sir,' Morgance spoke in O'Conner's raspy voice.

Bainbridge turned toward her, startled. 'Yes? Oh, it's you, Mr. O'Conner. Have you decided to join us then?'

'Join you?' Morgance, disguised as the old man, weaved back and forth uncertainly. 'Why, I'm just trying to get to my wife. She's a bit forgetful, y'know. And I'm afraid she's going to have an accident. See?' he added a bit more strongly. 'Look where she's gotten herself! Could you possibly help me bring her down from there?'

Blake looked over at the side of the ship where the old man had gestured. He gasped in horror. There, having gotten through the normally locked gate opened surreptitiously by Kostya, stood the frail little old woman known as Mrs. O'Conner, at the very top of the observation platform — with nothing between her and the open sea below but a flimsy half-railing.

'Oh my God!' Blake muttered. 'Yes,

145

come on. We should get help.'

'No! No! Please don't alert anyone else. She would be so embarrassed to make a scene. I think she just went up there to get a better look at everything. But I think I can talk her down all right. I'm just a bit uncertain of those steps.'

'Of course.' Blake lowered his voice and looked about. Everyone was still concentrating on Kenway, who was now waxing eloquent about how the Establishment was trying to ruin everything for all the Enlightened Ones. 'Come on,' he added, taking O'Conner's elbow, and wondering a bit at what seemed like extra padding under the jacket sleeve. 'Let's go. I'll help you.'

The two men, Blake favoring his gimpy leg, made their way as quickly as possible to the back of the group, then circumnavigated the railing until they reached the little gate. Morgance gave an slight nod to Kostya, standing in the shadows near a servers' entrance a few feet away, and he moved quickly back inside the ship.

'Now, up we go,' said Blake, trying to

sound confident. 'We'll soon have your wife down.'

With Blake's assistance, the old man struggled up the steep steps and stepped out onto the platform next to his wife. 'Dearest,' he said, 'you shouldn't be out here. It's not safe.'

'Oh, I'm just fine,' squeaked Nevin in Mrs. O'Conner's high peal. 'Isn't it beautiful up here? Look at the white caps!'

Morgance turned back to Blake. 'Give me your gun,' she demanded in her natural voice. '*Now!*'

'Wha . . . ?' Blake stared at her uncomprehendingly. 'What are you talking about?'

'I know you have a weapon on you,' she repeated. 'Give it to me. I need it — *now!*'

Blake looked about in confusion. 'I . . . I don't know . . . ' He felt about his waistband and pulled out the revolver and held it in his hand, staring down at it. 'What do you need it for?'

'We're in danger!' Morgance hissed at him, then turned toward the gallery below and called out in O'Conner's voice: '*Help! Help us please! This man is going to kill us!*'

Blake turned from Morgance to Nevin, still holding the gun, now aimed haphazardly in the direction of the old couple.

'What are you doing?' he asked plaintively. 'I was just trying to help . . . '

Morgance looked down at the crowd below and made sure that many, if not most of them, had noticed the little drama taking place on the platform.

'*Now!*' she cried to Nevin. 'Do it *now!*'

Both of the O'Conners made a little gesture, as if genuflecting, and stared back at Blake as if in disbelief. Suddenly, two loud reports rang out, one after the other. A blossom of red, like a chrysanthemum, spread out across Mrs. O'Conner's lacy blouse, and a moment later a similar pattern appeared on Mr. O'Conner's snowwhite shirt front.

Mrs. O'Conner wavered a bit in the bright sunlight, looking pained and a bit surprised, as if she had been caught unawares by a stranger. She fell up and over the low railing, her body convulsing as if, indeed, she had been shot like a villain in an old western film. As the crowd watched in horror, she tumbled over and over, and down and down, her skirt and blouse waving like pennants in the breeze — until they could see her no more.

Mr. O'Conner, in the meantime, had staggered toward the rail where his wife had gone overboard, and with one last cry of agony, pulled himself up and over and hurled himself toward the sea in her wake.

Blake Bainbridge stood gazing at the gun in his hand as if it were a thing of magic that he did not completely comprehend. He continued to stand there, transfixed, until the first few Foundation members reached him — and he did not offer any resistance when they took the gun from him and pulled him down to the deck below.

7

Nevin came to the surface first, choking and gasping for air. He only hoped he had swum underwater far enough away from Promenade Deck to avoid detection. He looked about, slightly panicked and disoriented. Yes! There it was, the nylon double-looped rope dangling from the huge anchor chain and just barely touching the surface of the water — just where Kostya had promised it would be. He swam heavily toward the side of the ship, taking care not to put himself in a position of getting slammed against it by the rolling breakers.

He felt almost naked, the water was so cold. And indeed, he had stripped himself of the trappings of old Mrs. O'Conner. At least he was free of that masquerade now. How he had hated mincing about, pretending to be someone and some*thing* he wasn't! He would almost rather be found out and captured than go back to that emasculating role once more.

The cold water was invigorating, however, and he was in no real danger of freezing, since Morgance had had the forethought to insist he don an abbreviated rubber wetsuit beneath the lady's long skirt and blouse. Once he had tugged the outer clothing away, he was free to swim beneath the waves and strike out for the front of the ship — all underwater, of course. Lucky he was a strong swimmer.

He looked about, trying to spy Morgance. A sudden fear struck him. What if she had not survived the jump? What would he do next? How would he function without her telling him what to do and when to do it?

Disgusted with himself, he struck out for the dangling rope and was startled when a slim hand reached out past him to grasp the lifeline.

'Morgance! Are you all right?' His teeth were chattering and he could hardly utter the words.

'I'm fine, you fool!' she shouted back at him. 'Come on, grab the rope. Kostya should be above to help haul us in.'

And, true to his word, just as they both had gained a secure handhold on the rope while balancing against the anchor chain, it slowly began moving upward, pulling them with it. It stopped once or twice as Kostya adjusted the electric winch, but he worked steadily and they hung on gamely, until at last, at a small landing about a third of the way up the front side of the ship, they were able to step onto a firm foothold. A hand reached out of an open porthole and assisted Morgance, followed by Nevin, into a small storage area in the hold of the ship. They stood there a moment, dripping and catching their breaths.

'What is this place?' Morgance asked, looking about speculatively.

'It's just a storage area,' Kostya answered shortly. He was pulling up the rope and winding it into a coil. 'They keep the ballast tanks full of water in these places along the bottom and sides of the ship. It's important that the weight is distributed evenly when there's little or no cargo in the hold. If there is too much weight on one side or the other, the ship could roll over and capsize.'

'Hmm.' Morgance eyed the ballast tanks more closely. 'How are they emptied?'

'Emptied? They just turn on those pumps over there. But it has to be done very carefully. Why?'

'Oh, just curious.' She shook out her hair in a golden frizz. She, too, had divested herself of all of Mr. O'Conner's outer clothing and stood there in sock feet, clad only in the form-fitting wetsuit. 'Just one of those pieces of information that might come in handy.'

★　★　★

Two of the captain's men led a dozen or so of the more vulnerable guests from the wedding party along a passageway toward the rear of the ship. Jones himself had decided he should stay with David and Richard and their men as they attempted to retake the ship.

Deborah kept glancing anxiously at Connie. He seemed very pale and short of breath. Definitely not a good sign.

'How are you doing?' she asked when he stumbled at one point. 'Do you need to stop?'

'No,' he panted. 'We've got to get someplace safe. I don't want to fall behind.'

'All right,' she agreed. 'But let me know if you need to rest. No point in pushing it.'

But suddenly, just as the little group turned a corner near their goal, two brawny men stood blocking their way.

'Let us pass,' demanded one of the officers. 'You have no business here!'

'Shut up!' shouted one of the intruders as they revealed their handguns, cocked and ready to fire. 'You stop right here or I'll blow your brains out!'

'What is the meaning of this?' The second officer stepped forward. 'What are you doing?'

'We've taken over the ship in the name of the Foundation and all it stands for!' The ruffian's eyes glinted with mad glee. 'You're all our prisoners now.'

So saying, he quickly searched the two

officers and removed their weapons. He then pulled their hands behind their backs and strapped them tightly with strong cords.

'Now,' he said to the rest of the company, shivering in fear, 'you're all coming with us.'

*   *   *

Wright Weatherby and Tate Zeeman landed at JFK in New York, collected their belongings and made their way down the concourse and out to the pick-up area at the front of the airport. Both were a bit jet-lagged, after their mad dash from the O'Conner residence to O'Hare and the flight being held for them.

'There it is.' Tate gestured toward a sleek black sedan parked a few places down the line of vehicles waiting for arrivals.

'Good. I hope we can get a chance for a quick shower and change,' Wright muttered. 'I could use a bite to eat, too.'

'Fat chance. The way this thing is

shaping up, we'll be lucky if we come to surface next week, let alone today.'

'Well, a guy can hope, can't he?' Wright wiped a big paw across his sweaty brow and nodded at the operative who had jumped out of the Seville to help them with their baggage.

'Agents Weatherby and Zeeman?' the young man asked, glancing at their IDs. 'I'm Agent James, Terry James. Have a good flight? I've been instructed to take you right to headquarters. Mr. Bainbridge is waiting for you there.'

Wright gave an 'oh well' shrug and hopped into the back seat, leaving the driver to deal with his bags. He leaned back in the comfy leather seat and waited while Tate oversaw getting their luggage in the trunk before joining his companion.

'So much for a shower and food,' he said as Terry checked traffic and moved the car smoothly away from the curb. 'Looks like we're in for it, if Bainbridge is already on board.'

They didn't speak further as they sped along Manhattan's busy streets. Finally

Terry signaled, then pulled into an underground parking garage, circled around to the elevators, and stopped.

'If you guys want to go on up, I'll deal with your bags. It's on the fourteenth floor, first suite of offices to your left.'

'Thanks, Terry. I'll take that one briefcase there. Yeah, the black one. It's got most of our notes in it. The rest of those things are okay. You can just leave them if we'll be driving to our hotel at some point.'

Terry handed Wright the case he'd pointed out, shook his hand, and got back in the car. 'See you later.'

'Yeah, thanks, Terry,' Tate added as he punched the 'up' button on the elevator panel. 'See you later on.'

The two agents entered the indicated suite of offices, where they were greeted by a tall grey-haired man in a dark suit. 'Hey,' he said. 'Did you have a good flight?' Without waiting for a reply he added, 'Would you like something to eat? Coffee?'

'No, Barry,' Wright said, easing onto a leather-covered sofa in the seating area. 'Let's get to it. I think we have a lot to discuss before we break for dinner.'

'You're right. Gentlemen, I'd like you to meet Blake Bainbridge, Sr. He's here because we think he may have some vital information that might give us some clues about the incident you uncovered in Illinois.'

Bainbridge, like his son, was an imposing figure. He had been handsome in his youth, and still retained the patrician good looks that only money and good breeding can secure. He was already seated in the one comfortable armchair in the room, and made no move to rise, although he nodded briefly at the two agents in greeting.

'On the evening of December twentieth,' Barry continued, 'two calls were placed to Mr. Bainbridge's home phone. No messages were left with the first call, but the second appears to have been from his son, Blake, Jr. Let me play it for you.'

He clicked a few buttons on a speaker phone, and the eerie disembodied voice of Blake Bainbridge, Jr. filled the room: ' . . . the *Nerissa* . . . tomorrow . . . good-bye . . . '

With the last word, Blake, Sr. bowed his head and closed his eyes in pain.

'So,' Barry said, clicking the tape into its 'off' position, 'what do you think?'

'Seems like a hell of a coincidence, doesn't it?' Tate rubbed his stubbly cheek. He felt sleep-deprived and stale, but this was a strange mystery. 'Doesn't really make any sense. Why would he kill that old couple in Illinois? What could his motive be?'

'Maybe it's part of a bigger plot; some sort of conspiracy.' Wright poured some water from the carafe on the coffee table in front of him. 'The only reason we found the victims so quickly is that they had scheduled a house-cleaning during their absence. When the woman let herself in the place was stinking to high heaven. She ran out and called the police.

'Now as far as we know, there was nothing missing except their suitcases, Mrs. O'Conner's purse, and Mr. O'Conner's wallet containing the couple's passports and tickets. We've been checking around, thinking that the thieves would try to cash them in at some point. We can't think what other use they'd have for those items, except if they had planned to sail on that particular ship. Hardly seems worth all the trouble they went to.

'And Blake, Jr. obviously didn't need the funds,' added Wright. 'He's already tapped into his old man's credit cards for all their worth. We're still tracking down all those charges. Nope, doesn't make any sense to me at all.' He took a deep slurp of water and set the glass down with a clink.

Blake, Sr. stirred in his chair. 'I can't understand it myself. All he had to do was ask. I would have gladly given him the money for a cruise, if that's what he wanted. Especially after all he's been through.'

'Yeah,' Barry interposed. 'We need to ask you about that. Part of our job is to establish a profile of the perp — excuse me, the person in question. If your son had any issues he was dealing with, problems real or imagined, stress in his life, we need to know that. And, sorry to say, we also need to know if he had any substance-abuse history. We're only concerned about getting to the bottom of this matter. Two people have been brutally murdered in their own home. We're not suggesting that your son had anything to do with it, but there is the coincidence that those tickets to sail on the *Nerissa* were stolen. And then your son left you that strange message which indicated he also was sailing on the same ship. Well, you can see our dilemma.'

'Yes, of course.' The older man wiped his forehead with a snow-white handkerchief before continuing. 'I can answer 'yes' and 'yes' to both your questions. Junior has been under a great deal of stress this last year, both physical and mental. And yes, he had been overusing his medications. But after attending a seminar a few months ago, he seemed to snap out of it some. He was more like his old self, cheerful and optimistic. But then . . . ' His voice trailed off and he reached for the handkerchief once again, this time to wipe his eyes.

'What was the reason for your son's problems, if I might ask?' Wright, senior of the two agents, took the lead.

'Last year — just before Christmas actually, so it was just about a year ago, in fact — he was involved in a head-on collision and nearly lost his leg as a result. Actually, we were just happy he survived the crash at all, but it has taken him most of the intervening year to regain use of the leg. The treatment and healing process was exceedingly painful and, of course, painkillers were prescribed.

'At first we thought nothing of that; anything to relieve his suffering and help him get back on the road to health again. But it soon became obvious that Blake . . . that Junior had a weakness for such things. He began requiring more and more, and when the doctors refused to increase his dosage, he went out on the street for it.'

'To your knowledge, is your son still addicted? And might he have stolen your credit cards in order to pay for his habit?' Tate hesitated, pen in air above his notepad, as he waited for the answer.

'Well, that's just it. This seminar, or whatever it was, took place several months ago. It seemed to work a miracle in him. For whatever reason, I do believe it worked; and what's more, I believe he is now free of his addiction. So no, I don't think that's the reason for the theft.'

'And in your opinion, is he capable of murder?' Wright paused. He hated to ask the question, but it had to be thrown out there.

Bainbridge, Sr. cleared his throat and looked away from Wright toward the skyline framed in the window beyond. After careful consideration he turned back to the two agents and spoke firmly: 'No, gentlemen. Under no circumstance do I think my son is capable of such a heinous act. Whatever may be going on, and whatever role he might be playing in this 'conspiracy,' there is no way Blake, Jr. would ever take another human being's life. Of that you may be assured.'

* * *

Back on board the *Nerissa*, Kostya confronted his two charges in the storage room. 'I think you should just hole up here until I can figure out what's going on. At least you'd be safe for the time being.'

'No, Kostya. I want you to take us back to our unregistered cabin. Now!' Morgance motioned towards the door leading into the passageway.

'I don't think that's wise.' Kostya's steely eyes challenged hers. 'We don't know who might be out there. We've been lucky so far. I don't want us to risk detection. It's foolhardy, and I don't advise it.'

'So you want to go off and leave us locked up here in this dung heap?' Morgance hissed at him. 'How do we know you won't turn us in, finish the objective yourself and collect our money? How can we trust you?'

'Morgance . . . ' Nevin began uncertainly. She was quirky all right, and unpredictable, but this was ridiculous. 'The man has just saved our lives. We would have died out there in the ocean if he hadn't helped us get back aboard.'

'And you . . . ' She turned accusingly to him. 'What have *you* been doing, except moaning and groaning and complaining every step of the way? Why must it always be me to make the decisions; make the hard choices?' She tossed her blonde mane. 'You're practically worthless to me!'

As she started purposefully toward the outer door to the compartment, Kostya stepped forward as if to stand in her way. Suddenly, and before either man could act, she whipped a small pistol out of a hidden pocket in her wetsuit, took careful aim and pulled the trigger.

With a discrete *pop* the gun exploded, and a single bullet flew across the intervening space and buried itself in Kostya's wide-open eye. He continued standing there for a moment more, looking as surprised as he had ever looked in his natural life, before crumpling slowly and inexorably, like a paper doll, into an untidy mass at Morgance's feet.

She bent and began systematically going through his pockets, removing a large key ring, his wallet, and a folded-up piece of paper. 'Ah! The schematics we will need to fulfill our mission!' She unzipped the top of her wet suit, stuffed everything inside, then pulled the zipper snugly up to her neck again. 'Come on,' she barked at Nevin, who recoiled from her in disgust.

'What did you do that for?' He backed into a corner of the room. 'We *needed* him! For God's sake, Morgance, what's *wrong* with you?'

She stood there for a second, staring at him coldly. 'Are you coming or not?'

He shrank back into the shadows, shaking his head. 'No!' he replied vigorously.

'Very well.' She reached toward the door handle. 'You're on your own, then. I won't be responsible for you any longer.' As she exited the room she threw back over her shoulder: 'Just don't interfere, understand? Stay out of my way!' And with that she was gone from his sight, and his life, forever.

★   ★   ★

Captain Robert Jones ('Call me Robbie,' he insisted) led his small group of men in the opposite direction of the party that included Deb and Connie. After a brief discussion, it was decided they would make their way through the servers' passageways until they could at least get a glimpse of what was taking place on the Promenade Deck.

'If we can find out where they're holding the rest of the crew, we may be able to free them and gain the upper hand,' the captain explained.

David and Richard agreed and they set off in silence, following the captain single-file through the dim corridors. What side-arms Jones and his men possessed had been distributed. They only hoped they could reach the locker in the control room before the cult members.

'If we can get those weapons,' Robbie iterated at one point, 'we'll have a better chance of regaining control of the ship.'

After a few minutes he paused, looked one way then the other, then ducked through a narrow doorway into an even dimmer and narrower area. 'Here,' he said gruffly. 'Let me check and see where we are.'

Gingerly, he pulled open a hatch-like door and peered out. Signaling to David, he stepped out cautiously into a protected area just beyond the open promenade. David followed, leaving the door slightly ajar behind him. The rest of the men huddled in silence in the close quarters.

'There!' mouthed Robbie close to David's ear. 'That's Trumball . . . but what's the matter with him? Looks like the woman has taken over.'

David peered around a large column, making sure to keep his face in the shadow and hidden. He watched as Amyas strode up and down in front of the rapt audience, her voice carrying across the deck seductively. 'And, my friends, if we can do *this* . . . well, then we can do *anything* we wish to do! And together we can change the world and bring peace and understanding to all mankind! We are in the new Millennium, and all the Power is now in our hands! Come now, all of you! Join us in this grand undertaking. Together we will make a new Future for us all. All money, all wealth, will flow to us, as the River flows to the Sea! All we have to do is will it, and it will happen. Here! Now! Right before our very eyes!'

She paused and took a deep breath.

There was a murmur of anticipation from the crowd. They had no idea what was being planned or what would be expected of them, but they were all for it.

David had no doubt that these idiots would follow Amyas and her crowd anywhere at this point, including off the top of the ship and into the icy sea below. He turned back to Robbie, who was standing there looking on in disbelief at what was happening to his shipshape existence. The other man looked back and shook his head.

'What do we do now? I think there's too many of them for our little party, especially with few weapons.'

David scanned the group, looking for any familiar face in the throng. He stopped. There, a few feet away, was Blake Bainbridge, hands cuffed behind him, and obviously being held against his will.

'See that?' He motioned to Robbie. 'Do you think we can grab him before anyone notices?'

'Why? Of what use is he to us?' Robbie was about to turn back into the doorway, but David put out a hand to stop him.

'I think he might make a good witness against these people, when and if we're able to regain control. At some point you and your company, not to mention the authorities, are going to want to bring the conspirators into court. It would be helpful to have an insider who might be 'persuaded' to testify for us.'

'I see what you mean,' Robbie agreed. 'But it could be a bit risky. Do you think we can pull it off?'

David surveyed the scene carefully. Blake's handler was standing just in front of him. He was watching the proceedings and paying no attention to Blake whatsoever, confident that he was securely bound.

'If I can pull him back quickly enough, you get that door open. If we can get him into the passageway and lock the door, I think we can do this.'

'All right,' Robbie said, nodding. 'Just try to make as little noise as possible.'

David crept stealthily forward until he was just behind Blake. He tapped the prisoner on the shoulder and when Blake looked around in surprise, David put a finger to his lips and gestured back at the doorway. Blake nodded and shuffled backwards a bit. The handler glanced sideways at him, but Blake stared stonily ahead and soon the guard turned his attention back to the speaker.

Quickly, David grabbed Blake by both elbows and steered him backwards across the deck toward the now-open passage door. Robbie and Richard were just inside and grabbed both David and Blake, dragging them to safety. Robbie slammed the door shut and bolted it securely.

'What are you doing? Are you going to hurt me?' Blake asked anxiously, looking from face to face.

'That's not our intention, but you're in our hands now,' David said. 'And if you know what's good for you, you won't give us any trouble.'

'God, no! I don't want any trouble with anyone!' Blake blubbered. 'All I want to do at this point is go home and beg my father's forgiveness. I've made a terrible mistake. I don't know if I can ever repair the damage I've caused.'

'Good!' David said. 'We're going to

give you that chance, starting right now. What can you tell us about this Foundation bunch, and what are their objectives?'

★   ★   ★

Morgance found the Hubèrts' unregistered cabin with no difficulty. She looked through the batch of master keys she had retrieved from Kostya, selected one, thrust it into the lock and the door sprung open.

Inside, she quickly ransacked the mini-fridge, pulled out a handful of snacks and a bottle of water, and flung herself into the chair in front of the desk. Eating a few snacks at random and drinking thirstily from the bottle, she pulled out the paperwork containing the satellite array passwords and more detailed schematics for the ship and perused it all carefully.

Finally, she gathered everything up again, found a plastic bag in one of the drawers, and stuffed everything inside. She visited the bathroom briefly and returned to the bedroom, still clad in the tight-fitting wet-suit. She was sweating profusely by now, and wanted nothing more than to strip down and take a long, hot shower.

But there was no time for that. She pawed through the drawer she had been using, pulled out a shapeless jogging outfit, and tugged it on over the wetsuit. It would restrict her motions, but she had no idea how the next few hours would play out. She might have to go back in the water at some point, and she wanted to be prepared.

She ran a brush through her frizzy mop and pulled it back away from her face. In the closet she found one of the small backpacks supplied by Kostya's people. She stuffed it as full as she dared, with two of the small bombs and detonators, the plastic bag of schematics, a handful of snacks and another water bottle. After adding a length of narrow nylon rope and leather gloves, she zipped it all shut and tested the heft. Not bad. She thought she could handle it with no difficulty.

She took out the small handgun and checked it for ammunition before replacing it discretely under the baggy shirt. After looking around the room for anything she might have missed, she switched off the light, opened the door a crack and peeked out into the hall.

Nothing there. Morgance slipped into the silent corridor and moved quickly toward the elevators. Time to make her rounds. It had occurred to her that with all the people rounded up by the Foundation, this would be an opportune moment to go through the more luxurious staterooms looking for cash, jewelry and credit cards. If the Russian Mafia threw her to the wolves, she might need such assets for a getaway.

And Morgance prided herself on being prepared for all possibilities — good and bad. It was who she was.

★ ★ ★

With his former companion now out of the picture, Nevin pondered his next move. He couldn't stay here, that was for sure. Not with Kostya's dead body lying there, accusing him silently of betrayal.

Why hadn't he interfered sooner?

174

Could he have wrested that pistol from Morgance's hand in time?

Well, there was nothing for it now but to get out and away from here as soon as possible. He looked about the storage area. Nothing here, really, that would be useful. And Morgance had gone through Kostya's pockets. She wouldn't have left anything there worth saving.

The only thing he could think to do was to try and find his way back to the O'Conners' stateroom. He was certain that Morgance would follow her first instinct and go to the unregistered cabin, believing that no one would think to look for them there.

So he would go to the O'Conners' room. If he could somehow force the lock, he might be safe there for a while. At least he could get his bearings, and get out of this wetsuit and into some regular clothing.

Clothing! He glanced over at Kostya's still form speculatively. Well, the man was definitely taller and heavier than Nevin. But the purser's uniform would provide a disguise of sorts. Maybe he could make it work, at least until he could get to the other cabin.

Grimacing with distaste, Nevin pulled and prodded at Kostya's clothing, rolling him first one way then the other, until the last items, his underwear, were free. He took everything, including the shoes, over to a waist-high crate in the corner and looked it all over carefully.

No way, really, to make any adjustments here. He would just have to throw everything on and hope he didn't look like some tiny doll dressed up in giant's clothing — at least until he could get back to the stateroom. Morgance had a sewing kit, tape and safety pins stashed there. He knew he could fix up everything with a little time.

He dragged Kostya's naked body into the gloom of the furthest corner, hoping that anyone looking in casually would not find anything amiss. Checking to make sure everything seemed ship-shape, he shut out the light and opened the door cautiously.

He did not allow himself to think about what all this meant, and how his future had been inevitably changed by this last bit of violence. He had always been a survivor. And now, with this new turn of events, he would need to survive once again.

8

'Let's go over this again, Blake,' David said. 'Just what do the Foundation members hope to achieve by taking over the ship?'

Blake stretched his arms and yawned. His leg was hurting badly. After being rushed along a series of corridors back to the conference room, he was feeling woozy and a bit distracted.

'When was the last time you ate?' Richard interrupted. 'Would you like to take a bit of a break and have a bite to eat? Coffee, maybe?'

'What I could use right now is some aspirin. Or something stronger, if you have it.' Blake gestured to his leg. 'This is hurting like a son of a gun. I usually take a pretty strong dose of aspirin every few hours. The pain makes it hard for me to think straight.'

'All right.' Captain Jones pulled out the meager first-aid supplies they'd gathered and began looking through. 'Here's aspirin, and there is a container of codeine . . . ' He hesitated uncertainly.

'No,' said Blake forcefully. 'No codeine. I need to keep my wits about me. The aspirin will do just fine. Two or three, if you can spare them.'

Robbie Jones poured out three tablets and handed them to Blake along with a bottle of water. He gulped them down eagerly and sat back with a sigh before continuing his story. 'Trumball and his top advisors are plotting to scuttle this ship near one of the lesser-known islands — '

'Scuttle the ship!' Jones shouted. 'Why the hell would they do that? Don't they realize they would be putting every passenger aboard, including themselves, at very grave risk?'

'I think that's part of the plan. Once they've determined just which of the passengers, and even crew members, are willing to throw in with them, they will set off a few selective charges. As the ship begins to sink, they will deploy as many lifeboats as necessary to take them and their followers away from the ship and on to the nearly deserted island nearby.'

'But *why*?' Blake's questioners were all gathered around him now in great concern.

'It's my understanding that there is a universal salvage law in effect on the high seas. Once the captain and his crew have either abandoned ship, or been 'dispensed with' in some other manner, the scuttled ship is fair game for anyone who can salvage her.'

'That's basically true,' admitted Jones. He was having difficulty keeping the anger from his voice. 'But what would be the purpose?'

'For money,' put in Richard. 'Pure and simple. If they have a salvage vessel standing by, it's possible they could make a very good haul from whatever they can take off the ship and its remains. If, as you say, they are able to get rid of any witnesses and make their own escape, the salvage people would pretty much have free rein. The other possibility is that they plan to hold the ship and its crew hostage for a big ransom from the cruise-line company. Either way, they could end up making a fortune off this, and that would finance their operations for years to come.'

'Yes,' agreed Blake. 'I think there was some talk of that as an alternative, in case they were unsuccessful with the first plan.'

'What I don't understand,' put in Carl, 'is how they thought they could convince all these people to go along with them. How many passengers are there on one of these liners, anyway?'

'Approximately three thousand, give or take, is the normal roster,' said Jones. 'But for some unknown reason, we ended up with considerably fewer on this particular cruise. There were a lot of last-minute cancellations. I think we ended up with less than half the usual complement. There was even some talk of cancelling the whole voyage, but the company decided they couldn't afford the negative publicity, so we went ahead.'

'Hmm.' David shook his head. 'I wonder if that was also part of the conspiracy. They could have made a lot of reservations, then called in cancellations at the last minute. I'm also wondering if a large number of the so-called passengers on this cruise are already members of the Foundation.'

'That would make sense,' said Richard. 'But that doesn't explain what happened with the O'Conners and what part they were supposed to play in all this.'

'I have no idea who they are — were,' said Blake. 'I don't think they were part of our group at all, but there was certainly something odd about them. And I know one thing for sure: I was not the one who killed them.'

'So you're sure your gun was never fired?' David asked. Blake shook his head, and David and Richard exchanged looks.

'You know what I think?' Richard said quietly. 'I think the whole thing was just a stunt to distract everyone. I don't think those two are dead at all. How far away is their cabin? Do we know which one it is?'

'I do,' replied David. 'I saw them going in and out several times. I think a couple of us should get over there and search it. Maybe they left some clues; something that would give us an idea of what we're dealing with here.'

'All right,' agreed Robbie. 'You and Richard take my master key and get over there right now. It's not far from here.' He pulled out the ship's diagram again and showed them the closest route to the state-rooms on that level. 'Meanwhile, the rest of us will start formulating some plans for taking back the control room. I don't know if we can prevent them following through on scuttling the ship, but I know damned well we're going to try!'

* * *

Nevin stood up and turned around in apprehension as the door to his cabin suddenly flew open and David and Richard stepped inside. All three men paused in silence to assess the situation.

Finally, Nevin cleared his throat and spoke. 'What is the meaning of this? Who are you to come barging into my room like this?'

'I think you know very well who we are, 'Mr. O'Conner,' or whoever you are,'

David began, but he stopped abruptly when the shiny nose of a revolver appeared in Nevin's clenched fist.

'Now, stop and think what you're doing,' Richard said smoothly. 'I'm sure we can figure this out. We were concerned about your safety. There have been reports that you and your wife had some sort of an accident up on the Promenade Deck.' He totally ignored the fact that Nevin no longer resembled either of the O'Conners. He also took great pains to look away from the weapon pointed at him.

'I'm not Mr. O'Conner, gentlemen,' began Nevin, but David interrupted him.

'Then who are you? I know this is the O'Conners' stateroom, but if you're not Mr. O'Conner, then why are you here?'

'Er . . . ' Nevin paused. He had no idea how he was going to worm his way out of this. He had been so thankful to rid himself of the dreadful O'Conner disguise that he had given little thought to how convenient it might be to continue carrying out the lie, at least until he could figure out what to do. If only Morgance

. . . But, no! He was not going to rely on that sick woman any longer.

Shaking, he lowered the gun and looked at the two men appraisingly. 'If I were to tell you what actually happened to the O'Conners, do you think you could look the other way; just let me go?'

'No,' David said coolly, stepping forward and relieving Nevin of his gun. 'No, we won't let you go, because I think you're a material witness to everything that's been happening on this ship over the past couple of days. But what I *will* do is this: I will make a statement to the authorities saying you have cooperated fully with us. Mr. Black Wolf, here, and I have been given leave to act in the captain's behalf, just until we get things sorted out. Now,' he added more gently, 'what can you tell us about this conspiracy to scuttle the ship?'

Nevin's eyes widened. 'I know nothing of such a conspiracy. My partner and I have been hired by . . . by an independent organization to make a slight adjustment to the satellite array in the communications room. We were to be paid a great sum of money to do this. Whatever else is going on,' he added, 'is a complete mystery to me. I have no idea who these other people are or why they are doing this. Our operation was a very small one in comparison, and certainly we had no plans to scuttle the ship.'

Richard and David looked at each other in concern. A second operation? To interfere with the ship's satellite communication system?

'Quick, and be as accurate as you can,' said David. 'Is your partner still on board? And do you think he plans to carry out the operation?'

'Yes. *She*'s still on board, and she is very dangerous. In fact, she has just killed the ship's purser down in one of the storage areas.'

'All right.' Richard motioned Nevin to sit down. 'You wait while we look through the room. There may be items here to assist us later on.'

As David began searching through the wardrobe and drawers, he noticed a strange object sitting on top of the dresser, surrounded by various make-up items and lotions. He picked it up and shook it. It rattled.

'What's this?' He showed it to Nevin. 'Is this of any significance?'

'It's a Russian puzzle doll,' Nevin said in disgust. 'Morgance — my partner — collects them, that's all. It is of no significance whatsoever.'

David stuffed the little doll into his pocket and turned to say something to Richard. But just at that moment there was a rumble and jerk. The ship was moving once more!

'Damn,' said Richard. 'They must have started the engines again. They're changing course!'

*   *   *

Morgance, too, had noticed the restarting of the engines. She had been making her way methodically through the deserted corridors of the upper plusher decks, stopping at each stateroom, entering with her master key, and quickly perusing the contents for easily transportable items like money, jewelry and credit cards.

She was disappointed and puzzled, though, when she discovered that many of the rooms were vacant and pristinely made up for future occupants. What had happened? This cruise should have been fully booked, given the holiday season and the cruise line's heavy promotion. Did this have anything to do with the takeover by the Foundation?

Finally tiring of her lack of success, she glanced at O'Conner's watch strapped to her forearm. She must get to the satellite room before the moment when she would need to input the information required by her handlers. She intended to make good on the promised payment if at all possible.

She stopped to peruse the schematics and get her bearings. Checking her watch again, she realized she would have just enough time to enter the main casino. Hopefully one of Kostya's keys would open the vault. There should be a windfall of cash in there. Once she had cleared the safe, she should be able to get to the satellite controls before the appointed hour.

She picked up speed, half-loping along the carpeted hallways. She was tired and would have liked nothing better than to have holed up in that safe room and slept for a while. But she dare not stop now. Fear and greed drove her on — and eventually she reached the casino deck and entered the tall swinging doors leading into the large hall beyond.

She allowed a moment for her eyes to adjust to the darkened interior, then began moving slowly around the perimeter of the room toward the cashier's cage. The vault — *a* vault — must be there. And it should — *must* — be loaded with cash. She was prepared to empty her backpack of everything but that golden treasure trove she hoped to find at the end of this particular rainbow.

'Stop!' a woman's voice rang out, and Morgance halted in her tracks in terror. No! This couldn't be happening now. Not when everything had been going so smoothly.

Looking around, she could just make out a faint form hovering in the darkness near the bar. 'What do you want?' she called out. 'I'm just looking for something to eat.'

The woman stepped out of the shadows and moved into view. It was Amyas, that woman from the cult — and she had a revolver in her hand pointing straight at Morgance's head.

'Don't move,' Amyas said. 'Put down your bag and put your hands up.'

'Why?' Morgance, no stranger to disguise, put on her most innocent face and tried to look stupid. 'I've done nothing wrong. I'm just a passenger, looking for something to eat. There seems to be something wrong with the service. I can't find anyone to help me.'

'You don't fool me one bit,' Amyas replied. 'I've been watching you, and I know who you are. You and your partner have something to do with the O'Conners — and I want to know what you've been up to.'

'You're wrong,' Morgance insisted. 'I don't know what you're talking about.' She had dropped the bag all right, but her gun was still tucked into her waistband, slightly under and behind her free right hand. 'Look,' she added, 'I'm beat. I've been roaming around this ship all afternoon looking for food and something to drink. Do you mind if we move to that table over there?' She gestured. 'We can talk about it sitting down, at least.' She tried to sound exhausted, which she was, and ended on a plaintive high note.

'All right,' Amyas agreed. 'But stay where I can see you.'

Morgance made a quick decision. She figured that Amyas did not see her as a real threat; and the cult woman had no idea, of course, that Morgance was armed. She began to move in the direction of the table, then stumbled and caught herself. As she came up, her right hand whipped around to her right, almost as if she had a sudden stitch in her side — but the gun came out blazing. The three shots that rang out in the cavernous room caught Amyas first in the right hand, knocking her gun away. Next, a crimson stain appeared above her left breast where the second bullet nicked the artery leading from her heart. The final bullet left a neat round hole right in the middle of Amyas's forehead.

The lady was dead before she hit the floor.

Morgance looked at her coldly. *Served the bitch right,* she thought, *trying to interfere with me. Guess I showed her what's what.*

Hastily, she went through Amyas's pockets and stripped her of her jewelry. Checking the revolver and noting it was still fully loaded, she jammed it into her waistband next to her own gun and ran back to retrieve her pack.

Urgently now, she made her way to the cashier's cage, fingered through her master key ring until she found one that looked right, thrust it in the keyhole, and opened the cage. There it was — a heavy steel vault taking up a good part of the rear wall. Hopefully it could be opened with a master key, not a combination.

She was in luck; the key was easily recognizable. She could have laughed out loud at the stupidity of the cruise line's owners. No combination! What a joke!

She spun the handle and pulled the heavy door open. There, to her wondering eye, lay stacks upon stacks of currency, in various denominations; to her great delight, in Euros as well as American dollars. She emptied her bag of everything and began cramming in the bound notes as tightly as possible.

When she had packed as much as she thought she could carry, she glanced through the jewelry, picking out the pricier pieces and stuffing them down in the crevices among the notes. Amyas's diamond studs and ring were among them. The rest of the items she swept into a bucket she noticed sitting in a corner of the cage. If she had time after changing the satellite settings, she would come back and retrieve the rest of the loot. *If* she had time.

★   ★   ★

When David and Richard returned to the others with Nevin in tow, they began questioning him in earnest. Blake, sitting in silence across the room, looked on in amazement as Nevin outlined exactly what he and Morgance had been doing since they had boarded the ship, how they had staged their own deaths, and finally, how Morgance had killed their handler in cold blood.

'After that,' he said numbly, 'I just kind of gave up. I'm sick of the violence. At this point, I just want to turn myself in and get what's coming to me.'

'If you cooperate with us like Blake here,' David assured him, 'we'll do everything in our power to make sure you get a fair trial. That's all we can promise you. I hope you'll agree to assist us rather than cause problems.'

Nevin reflected. He had not breathed a word about what he and Morgance had done to the real O'Conners. He was trying to think through how he might worm his way out of a murder charge by testifying against Morgance in the conspiracy plot.

'I agree,' he said. 'I don't want any further trouble, and I'll stay out of your way as much as possible. I promise you won't need to worry about me interfering with you now. If I can help in any way, I will. But I assure you I won't be any trouble to you.'

'Fine,' said Robbie. 'I'm suggesting we don't bind either Nevin or Blake,' he added to David and Richard, who nodded in agreement. 'We don't have time to play nursemaids right now. If the Foundation has started up the ship again, I suspect they are changing course. Probably took them this long to reconfigure the computers. They must have coordinates to the rendezvous with the salvage ship in place now. I thought I heard the anchors being raised a short while ago, too. We're definitely underway.'

'So should we make an attempt on the control room?' asked Richard. 'Or do you think our best bet is to try and free the other passengers and crew? What do you guys think?' He looked around at the other men in the room. 'Ideas?'

'My own thought is that we should try and get into that control room and take back control of the ship.' Robbie scratched his head in thought. 'There's those weapons in there, too, if they haven't already confiscated them.'

David paused. His own thoughts, of course, were with Deb, Connie and the others. Blake had been able to tell them where he thought the prisoners were being held. And there was the element of surprise. The thugs guarding the prisoners probably would not be expecting an attempt to free them.

'I think we need to get those prisoners freed first and foremost,' David said with confidence. 'It's the right thing to do, and we could use any extra help we can get.'

'Show of hands?' asked Robbie, looking around the room. Slowly, one hand after the other, including Blake's, went up.

'All right, then, let's do it. Blake, you okay to travel?'

'Yes, sir,' the young man answered stoutly. 'I'm with you.'

'Good. Let's go kick some butt!'

And one by one, including Nevin and Blake, they all filed out of the room.

★   ★   ★

Kenway Trumball had agreed with Amyas that he would make an effort to get himself in hand and take over controlling the people on the Promenade Deck while

196

she went to oversee resetting their course.

As the *Nerissa* had gotten underway again, he breathed a sigh of relief. She'd done it! God, he was lucky to have someone like her to help run things. He could see now that this operation had turned into something much more complicated than any of them could have anticipated.

But shortly now, just as soon as they had reached their destination near that deserted island way off the beaten path, and they had set off the final detonations that would scuttle the ship, killing all who remained aboard locked below decks, they would be clear and free. The salvage ship operator was sworn to secrecy. He would claim the wreckage; and whatever he got, either salvage or ransom from the cruise-ship line, would be split with the Foundation. The Swiss bank account was already set up, and already much of the donation money from contributors had been deposited there.

Yes, once all this took place, he and Amyas could start their new lives together — and they would be wealthy beyond their wildest dreams.

A little worm of worry niggled about his brain. There was the situation with Blake. Amyas had done her duty there — almost too willingly, he thought. And then there was the father. Would he continue to believe Blake had acted alone to steal his credit cards?

Oh well, it was fortunate in some ways that there had been that bizarre incident with the older couple. He didn't believe for an instant that Blake had actually shot them before they went overboard. One of his people had been taping the proceedings for posterity, and for the lucrative film he hoped to produce at some point under an alias, of course.

When they reran the tape, it was quite clear that Blake's gun had not gone off at all. It looked very much as if the explosions had been planted in the couple's clothing. But why? He couldn't figure out what their motive was. Were they just trying to thwart the takeover? And if they weren't killed by the gun, what had happened to them? Was it just an elaborate suicide plot?

He shook his head and turned back to his followers, all smiles, and giving them a thumbs-up sign of approval. He mustn't allow his misgivings to shadow the success of this day.

They finally were on their way! And he and Amyas would soon be together in paradise forever.

★ ★ ★

Morgance turned a sharp corner in the passage and stopped short. Just ahead of her, back turned, was an armed guard blocking the entrance to the satellite room. She wasn't surprised, just disappointed. She had hoped the conspirators were so involved with other issues that they would have forgotten this area.

Regrouping, she slid, back to the wall, out of sight. Bending over to catch her breath, her mind raced. Time was running out and her sleep-deprived brain was not functioning as sharply as it should.

What could she do to distract them? Remembering what Kostya had told her, an edge of an idea began to form. The ballast! If she could manage to turn the big valves in the ballast room, she could empty the ballast water out of the tanks on one side of the ship, causing it to list. The takeover crew might be so confused that they would call on every hand to investigate. The consternation caused by the danger to the ship might give her the edge she needed to carry out the rest of her mission.

Back to the hold she ran, oblivious now to anything but the urgency of time. Once back in the room, she glanced uncaringly at Kostya's body crumpled in the corner. So Nevin had made use of the uniform. She grinned at the thought of the little man, sleeves and pants legs rolled up, trouncing about the ship like a tiny Napoleon.

She quickly found the main valve she was looking for, grabbed a nearby crowbar which had apparently been used for this procedure, and bent into her task. Slowly, slowly, the valve began to creak open, and she could hear the water in the ballast on the port side slowly being sucked out into the ocean. Once the valve had been opened up completely and she was sure the water was leaving the ship, she turned around and dashed back to the satellite area. As she ran, she began to feel the ship adjust slightly, then suddenly list sharply to one side.

Sure enough, as she reached the corner nearest the communications corridor and peered around, she could see two of the guards, assault rifles looped over their arms, speaking earnestly into the receivers strapped to their shoulders. After a moment of discussion, they turned abruptly and ran in the opposite direction.

She stepped cautiously around the corner, moved to the door and looked in. There, in all its glory, sat a large computer mounted to the communications console. Complicated connections led to a battery of equipment including, she assumed, the satellite array.

She crept forward, pulled out her sheet of instructions, and after a moment to get her bearings, began calmly to enter a series of instructions to turn the array in the direction of the Russian satellite. Once completed, her part in this madness was done, and she could contact the mob for the rest of the money. She doubted that Nevin would interfere with any of her plans for it. She knew he was afraid of her now; afraid of what she was capable of doing, should she be crossed.

She stood back, marveling at the technology in front of her. She had no idea what information she had just communicated to the satellite hurtling through space, or what the results might be; but she didn't care. As long as she was paid for her work, she had no thought or feeling about what she might have set in motion for the rest of the world.

9

Wright and Tate, together with a selected group of combined FBI and CIA agents, had thrown protocol to the winds and were now gathered in a situation room on the coast of Florida.

'Any more news about the *Nerissa*?' Tate asked one of the young men running messages back and forth.

'Nope. All we know is they missed their first port of call — on Christmas Day, no less.' The man mopped his brow. He had been on duty for more than 10 hours now, with no end in sight. 'Do you guys need any more coffee here?'

'If I have any more coffee,' Wright growled, 'I'll never be able to look a mug in the face again! I could use some fresh bottled water though, when you have a chance. You look like you need to take a break yourself.'

'I'm OK.' The messenger smiled. 'Just getting my second wind. This is an interesting case, isn't it?'

'Interesting? Yeah, you could say that.' Wright grimaced. 'Interesting and frustrating combined. We have no idea what's going on aboard that ship, much less what any of the motivations are. We could use some sort of a breakthrough.'

Just then a little flurry of activity commenced on the other side of the room. As Wright and Tate looked up, the door was flung open and a Homeland Security agent entered the room with Blake Bainbridge, Sr. in his wake. 'Attention, people!' he called out. 'We've just had a sighting of the *Nerissa*. She's way off course, but is very near one of those little almost-deserted islands. Some guy out taking a joyride in his little private jet spotted her. He says it looks like she's lost power and is listing badly. She might be about to capsize. Fortunately, San Carlito Cay, as it's known, is a U.S. protectorate and thus under our jurisdiction. We've been able to get the Federal District Court's approval to proceed with the investigation.'

Wright and Tate exchanged looks.

Wright raised his hand.

'Yes?' The agent nodded at Wright.

'Thank you, sir. Under the circumstances, I think we need to send a team out there to the island right away. We know for a fact that two of the people who were supposed to be on that ship were murdered in their own home a day before the *Nerissa* left Florida. It was staged to look like an accidental death, but the forensic science just doesn't add up. They most likely were killed somewhere else and their bodies brought back and staged in their home to prevent suspicion for as long as possible. What's more, their cruise tickets and passports were stolen, so we believe the killers may have sailed on the *Nerissa*.

'We also believe there is a third party, Mr. Bainbridge's son, aboard. He is . . . unstable.' Wright glanced in sympathy at Bainbridge, Sr. 'And we think he also may have become involved in some sort of criminal activity. We've been unable to determine if there is a connection between the killing in Illinois and Mr. Bainbridge, but if the *Nerissa* is indeed in trouble, there may be a possible pirating or sabotage operation taking place. If so, all the other innocent passengers, not to mention crew members, are in jeopardy.'

There was a murmur of assent throughout the room, and the senior agent nodded. 'I believe you are correct in your assessment of the situation,' he said, 'and that all jibes with what we've been able to find out. Ordinarily we would let the Coast Guard handle this solely as a rescue mission. But with the other unknowns, well . . . I hate to be blunt, but we at Homeland Security are looking at the very real possibility of international terrorism. There is too much we don't know, and we've been unable to contact the ship through usual channels. For some reason their communications systems seem to be off-line. Just another reason for our concern. Suggestions and comments?'

After a spirited back-and-forth discussion about their options and the possible international legal issues, it was decided that Homeland Security would notify Contessa and the Coast Guard of their intentions, and seek their approval and assistance in the investigations.

Wright and Tate were among the experienced agents chosen for the San Carlito operation, as it was dubbed, and with a few quick preparations they found themselves trotting across the tarmac to a waiting helicopter that would land them in a short while on the all-but-deserted islet nearest the disabled *Nerissa*.

'Still didn't get that steak dinner I was looking for,' groused Wright, pulling himself up through the open bay.

'You'll enjoy it all the more once we've put this case to bed,' shouted Tate above the roar of the rotors.

* * *

'Here, this way,' whispered Robbie urgently, leading the rescue party toward the deck where the hostages were being held. 'Careful, now — we want to keep the element of surprise.'

As quietly as possible, he unlatched the door leading from the servers' corridor to the back portion of the deck. He stood aside to allow his men to slip, one by one, out into the shadowy area under an unlit portico. Several, including Blake and Nevin, he ordered to stay behind in the passageway.

'We don't want to show too many of us all at once,' he whispered to David, motioning to the half-dozen men deployed behind the decorative pillars lining the deck.

The hostages were gathered in small groups, some seated in lounge chairs, and a few lying on blankets hastily thrown on the floor of the deck. There appeared to be only a small number of guards, but each carried an automatic weapon. This would not be easy.

David was alarmed when he spotted Deb and Connie in the group. 'Looks like our people didn't get away after all,' he said to Robbie. He was concerned to see that she was in earnest conversation with the leader of their captors.

'What's she doing?' asked Richard, directly behind him. 'Do you think she's trying to negotiate for Connie's release? He doesn't look so good.'

And, indeed, Connie was leaning

heavily on Deb's sturdy arm, his face pale and his body shaking convulsively. As David watched in concern, the guard shook his head at Deb and turned away from the two prisoners.

'I count seven guards in all,' said Carl. 'We could probably get a man behind each one and take them, if we're lucky and nobody notices us.'

'I think that's our best bet,' agreed Robbie. 'Once we begin acting, I know the hostages — the crew members at least — will act on their own. We just might be able to pull this off.'

'All right,' David agreed. 'Let's do it.'

Creeping back to the portico, he quickly assigned targets to each of his men. They began to fan out around the area, taking care to stay well in the shadows and out of sight. Once they were all in place, Robbie counted down and gave a silent hand signal. Their movements were swift and sure.

He was right. Once his crew members realized what was happening, they joined in with gusto. Soon all seven guards were seated back to back on the deck floor, their arms and legs bound together tightly, without a shot being fired. They then were searched for weapons, which were confiscated and redistributed amongst the rescuers.

'Seven in one blow!' crowed Richard. 'I think we did it!'

'Now we need to get better organized,' Robbie said. 'Determine which of these people need medical assistance and get more supplies gathered. Then we'll see what we can do about taking back control of the ship.'

Just then the captain was interrupted by an abrupt settling of the *Nerissa* itself. 'My God!' he exclaimed. 'Something's terribly wrong! I think we're sinking!'

★ ★ ★

Morgance loped back along the maze of corridors leading from the hold to the upper decks. It was difficult to maintain her balance as the ship continued to list and jerk violently. Her sleep-deprived mind was whirling, going over again the fortune of bank notes strapped in her backpack, the funds awaiting her in the

Swiss account, and one last thing: the tiny Russian nesting doll she'd left sitting on the dresser in the O'Conners' stateroom. She must retrieve it before saving herself. It was the only thing now that linked her to the brutal slayings in Illinois. But that wasn't the only reason. She *wanted* it. It was hers, after all. Spoils of war. And this *was* war; *her* war against all the things which had held her back in the past: poverty, lack of family, the nuns's cruelty in the convent orphanage. Yes, by God! She would risk stopping for the *matryoshka*. It was a symbol of all she had accomplished; all she had won in this battle between her and the rest of an uncaring world.

She was panting, and sweat was dripping from her face and down the back of her neck, by the time she reached the cabin. Without thinking she thrust the master key into the lock and rushed into the room. Flicking on the overhead light, she stopped in horror.

The stateroom had been tossed! Someone had been here before her, turning things over and leaving a mess. Drawers had been left open and the closet door stood ajar. She knew, almost before she looked, that the little doll was gone from the dresser top.

'No!' she screamed. 'No! No! No!' She picked up a heavy lamp and flung it at the mirror, which shattered into bits. She looked at her riven image in the remains. She resembled a Picasso-like cubist portrait, her frizzed hair standing on end and her wild eyes staring in different directions on either side of a sharp black gash.

She took a deep breath and went calmly into the bathroom, where she wet a cloth and wiped her face clean and dried it on the hand towel. The ship was buckling and bumping wildly now, but she carefully applied make-up to her ravaged visage. She didn't bother to run a brush through her frizzed hair, but left it pulled back away from her face and covered it with a dark ball cap. Smoothing her rumpled clothing and checking her backpack, she took another quick look around the cabin, shut off the light and returned to the hallway.

It was time to make her getaway.

★   ★   ★

The Promenade Deck was not as crowded as it had been earlier. This time Robbie, Dave and Richard moved purposefully at the head of a well-armed team. Those in the lead carried the assault weapons recently liberated from the hostage guards, followed by all crew members and passengers able-bodied enough to fight.

'All right!' Robbie shouted as they quickly overcame the weak resistance presented by the cult members. 'Let's show these suckers!'

Kenway crumpled to the deck with a whimper. 'Amyas!' he called out, but she had disappeared.

Once more the rescuers set themselves to the task of identifying those who were in need of medical care, and those who had been swept up in the cult frenzy without actually realizing what that meant. Hardcore members of the Foundation were separated and a guard was set over them.

As the ship listed further and further to

213

the left, Robbie urgently pulled together his most experienced crew members and set off with them for the control room. They expected little resistance in the smaller quarters, and he only hoped they would not be too late to right the sinking ship.

Just as Robbie and his men left, David was horrified to see a thin column of smoke rising up through one of the portholes.

The ship was on fire!

Urgently, David pulled together another detail headed by Carl and Chip, and sent them off to investigate and see if there was any possibility of putting out the fire.

The ship's medical officer could not be found and it was supposed he had been taken with some of the others to the control room. Deb began querying the passengers about their medical experience and lined up several to help her in assessing those in need of immediate treatment.

Her main concern was with Connie. She suspected his heart was acting up, but without access to any testing equipment, she could only treat his symptoms. She had already given him several doses of aspirin, and now urged him to sit quietly and try to relax as much as possible.

'As soon as we find the doctor, he might be able to make a better diagnosis,' she told him. 'I don't want to do anything that might make things worse.'

'I'll be all right,' he assured her, even as he lay back in a deck chair, his face ashen, his skin cold and clammy.

Richard and some of the ship's officers were questioning the passengers carefully, looking for signs of deception before they were cleared to join the others. 'How did you come to be here with Kenway's group?' he asked a young woman dressed in loose exercise clothing with a cap pulled down over her slicked-back hair.

'I'm not sure,' she said hesitantly. She smiled shyly and something about her seemed familiar. Possibly he had seen her in one of the lounges earlier.

'I was going to go to the gym,' she continued. 'But I guess I took a wrong turn and ended up here. There was all this talking and commotion going on. I just got confused and decided to wait until everything died down before I tried to find my way back to my cabin.' She smiled at him again.

'Go on over there with them.' He pointed toward the cleared passengers. She certainly looked harmless enough, and she didn't appear to have any idea about the cult or its objectives.

She quickly made her way across the deck and melted into the crowd gathered near the main exit.

Chip and Carl ran back on to the deck and got David's attention. 'It's out of control!' Carl reported. 'I don't know how long we've got, but if the captain can't get the ship righted again, I think we'd better start looking at getting off this bucket!'

Richard had finished evaluating the prisoners and joined them. 'I think those are all we can be sure of. I suggest we start trying to get them off first; wait until last for the idiots who started this mess.'

'I agree,' said David, turning to Jones's officers and men. 'How many people can we get in each lifeboat?'

'With the new double-deck fiberglass boats, three hundred, give or take,' replied

Robbie's second-in-command. 'And we have sixteen of them stowed on C Deck. We should only have to deploy half of them to handle everyone, including the crew. We'll have to move these people down there quickly, though,' he added, 'because of the ship listing. I just don't know how that's going to affect lowering the boats via the davits.'

'I don't think it's safe to use the elevators,' another officer said. 'But I think if we hurry, we still should be able to get most of these people off.'

'Let's go,' shouted David. 'Everyone — we need to get down to C Deck immediately and begin putting you off in the lifeboats!'

Grim-faced, the passengers, followed by most of the crew, began moving through the exits leading to the stairway. Those with medical difficulties or other handicaps followed in the company of Deb and her medical team. The cult prisoners, closely guarded by David's men, were kept well away from the others. They would be the last ones put off the ship.

As they were filing down the stairwell, the ship buckled again and several people fell.

'Hold on to the railing, everyone,' Richard called out. 'Try to keep your balance.'

Just before the last of them had left the Promenade Deck, Robbie Jones returned from the control room with a handful of people.

'It's no use,' he said, grim-faced. 'Not only has the port ballast been completely emptied, but in the process of changing course those idiots have screwed up the computers. I tried, but there's no way we can get back on line soon enough to save us.' He shook his head angrily.

'Do you think we can still deploy the lifeboats?' David asked anxiously. He kept glancing over at Deb, shepherding Connie down the steps. 'At least enough so we can get most of the passengers off?'

'It's going to be close, but we'll give it our best try,' Robbie said. 'I guess it was a blessing in disguise that we're not carrying a full complement. We thought it was strange we had so many cancellations just before sailing. I think now it was part of this insane plot to take over the ship. I actually think a good many of the passengers were plants.'

David nodded. 'Yeah, that's what Blake said. And you know, they just might have carried it off if it hadn't been for that crazy stunt pulled by Nevin and his partner. I wonder what's happened to her,' he added, looking over the group. 'Would be hard to spot her if she's disguised herself again.'

'I honestly don't care at this point,' muttered Robbie. 'I'm losing my ship, and we're not out of this safely yet. We can only hope we've been spotted by the Coast Guard. The communications computers were all messed up, too. No way to get word out.'

'Do you think there's any land around here?' Richard had pulled back to join them. 'Maybe we can find a deserted island.' He attempted to smile at his lame joke.

'Actually, there might be,' said Robbie. 'There's plenty of tiny dots of land in these waters, some of them not even charted because they're completely inundated with water periodically.'

'I wonder if that's what they had in mind — the conspirators, I mean,' David said. He glanced at Kenway being herded along between two armed crew members. 'I think I'm going to have a little talk with that guy.'

He made his way to the back of the line where the prisoners were being held. 'Mr. Trumball.' David hunkered down next to the completely cowed self-styled guru. 'I need to ask you some questions, and I expect you to answer honestly and completely, otherwise I can't vouch for what any of my men here may do.'

'Er . . . yes, sir.' Kenway's eyes shifted to David's. 'I'll do my best.'

'Good. We'll have less trouble that way.' David wasn't beyond threatening this piece of crap. He had put all of their lives in jeopardy, and David understood that it would be a miracle if they all survived the move off the ship.

'First of all, did you have any kind of game plan for what you were going to do once you had taken over the ship?'

Kenway hesitated. If Amyas were here, she'd know what to say and do. But he had not caught a glimpse of her either among the other prisoners, or with the freed hostages being taken down to the lifeboat stations. He shrugged. 'Of course,' he answered simply. 'Of course there was a *game plan*. We weren't complete fools, you know.'

'Did you have a rendezvous planned with another ship? Or did you change the coordinates deliberately to take us to some other location?' David scowled at Kenway before continuing. 'Think carefully now. If I turn you over to those men and let them know you planned for us all to die here, I will be very happy to stand back and let them have their way with you.'

'No!' Kenway begged. 'No, I'll cooperate. Our plan all along was to change course. Then, when we had reached a certain destination, we would scuttle the ship and . . . ' He cleared his throat. 'The plan was to scuttle the ship, take all the followers off in the lifeboats, then . . . '

'Leave us to die. That was your plan all

along, wasn't it?' David said disgustedly. 'But where were you going to go from here? You couldn't possibly expect to get away with this.'

'Oh yes, we were sure we would. There is one of those deserted islets nearby. We planned to make our way there on the lifeboats and wait for rescue, once it was known the ship had gone down. Meanwhile, a salvage ship operated by one of the Foundation members would steam in and claim the remains of the *Nerissa* for salvage. Or, if that wasn't possible, they would attempt to obtain a ransom or reward from the Contessa Lines owners. Our goal was not only to bring in more converts to the organization, but at the same time make money on the salvage project. It was foolproof.'

'Oh, yeah, it was foolproof, all right.' David shook his head in disbelief. 'How in God's name did you ever expect to pull off this idiotic scheme? Don't answer that,' he added. 'All I want to know now is if you have any idea where this deserted island of yours is. If we can get everybody into the lifeboats, and *if* we can get them lowered, given the listing of the ship, maybe you can buy yourself a little leniency.'

There was a short silence while Kenway weighed his options. Without Amyas, he no longer cared.

'Get me something to write on,' he said finally. 'I'll tell you exactly how to find the island.'

★   ★   ★

As the first full boatload of passengers began to descend into the sea, the automatic davits straining with the weight, Robbie, David and Richard discussed the order in which people would be taken off the doomed *Nerissa*. They figured it would take two more boats to accommodate the remaining passengers who were not part of the Foundation group.

'The rest of the women and injured, regardless of affiliation, should go in the next boat,' argued Richard. 'I don't want to be party to any deliberate attempt to punish anyone just because they've made some bad choices.'

The other two men reluctantly agreed, David thinking especially of Doreen, who had stayed with the cult members by choice. He was sure, with help, most of them could be rehabilitated.

'All right,' he said. 'But if we're going to do that I think we should include the men as well. I don't want to see anybody die just because they had some issues in their lives and chose to follow that fool.' He jerked his head toward Kenway, who was speaking earnestly to one of the shipboard navigators, trying to explain just where they would find land.

Once the decision was made, it was much easier to get people divided into the necessary numbers. Because of the larger capacity of the new, improved lifeboats, coupled with the decidedly low passenger count, they realized they would be able to get everyone off safely in just six boats.

Robbie demanded that he and his senior officers be allowed to wait for the last boat, and David, Richard and their men asked that they, too, be given that option, even though they were technically passengers and could have asked to leave with their loved ones.

A commotion at the front of the line drew their attention. Deb had pulled Connie out of line and was peering at him anxiously.

'What's wrong?' Dave demanded, rushing to her side.

'I think he's having a heart attack!' she said hoarsely. Her face was ravaged with strain, lack of sleep and concern. 'I think we'd better get him lying down.'

They placed him on the floor and tried to cushion his head. 'Come on, old man,' Dave said encouragingly. 'Just a few more steps and you'll be on that boat and on your way to safety. Don't give up on me now.'

Connie reached up and patted Dave's cheek. 'You were always my best boy, Davie. You were the son I never had. Do me proud, now, hear?'

As Dave gazed into his old mentor's eyes, he saw the pupils enlarge as if concentrating on something in the far distance. It was a look he was familiar with, and he waited a moment before checking the old man's pulse. He closed the lids of the staring eyes and turned to Deb.

'He's gone, Deb. Connie's gone!' Dave's voice cracked and he angrily wiped a tear away from his cheek. 'We can't do any more for him now. Let's get you off this crate.'

★　★　★

The choppers landed in a clearing hidden away from the white-sand beach on the deserted island known as San Carlito Cay. Despite its designation, there were perhaps half a dozen inhabitants of the tiny bit of coral and sand jutting up out of the Pacific, but their huts were located further inland, on the leeward side. With luck, they would never learn of the little drama that was playing out in the breakers on the ocean side.

Quickly the FBI agents and Homeland Security specialists set up ops and a medical triage, and prepared to intercept the first of the six lifeboats now barely visible on a heading in to shore.

'How will we know if they're part of the

takeover party or merely innocent passengers being rescued?' asked agent Powell, one of the younger members of the team.

'We *won't* know,' Wright explained. 'We'll have to question all of them and try to make that determination. We have no idea what has happened during the last few hours on that ship. It could have gone either way.'

'What we *do* know,' Tate added, 'is that there are several trained police officers aboard, not to mention the ship's own security contingent. I don't think they have a lot of weapons at their disposal. But, who knows? If they figured out soon enough what was going on, they might have been able to get a handle on it in time to rescue at least some of the passengers.'

'Given the capacity of those new-issue lifeboats,' said Homeland Security agent Keen, 'they should be able to get everyone off, if they're lucky. They weren't carrying at full capacity, which makes a big difference.'

Keen placed his men strategically

around the perimeter of the pristine beach, and they settled back to wait.

★ ★ ★

Deb stayed back with Dave while the next two lifeboats were loaded. 'After all,' she argued, 'I can't help Connie any more, and I'd rather stay a little longer with you. Let me wait until the last boats go down before I leave.'

He said nothing, but gave her hand a squeeze. They were all bone tired by now, having exerted much energy over the last few hours. If they could just get everyone off the ship before it went down, he would worry about everything else later.

Finally, there were only two boats left to load. The last boat would take the most violent of the cult guards and the remaining senior officers. When Robbie quit the ship, there would be no one left behind. He was insisting on that, and nobody said a word about it. He had proven himself during the ordeal, and he had earned the right to stay until the end.

There were only a handful of civilian

passengers who had chosen to wait to leave on this boat. Among them, Richard couldn't help but notice the young woman from the Promenade Deck. He wondered why she had elected to stay longer than necessary, but shrugged. It was her option, after all.

David watched impatiently until he saw Deb safely board the boat from the deck. These new lifeboats were engineered so that they could be lowered directly into the sea with electrically driven davits. The older models had to be swung out away from the side of the hull and took much longer to deploy.

The hatches were secured and soon the humming motors indicated the cables were being lowered.

Suddenly there was a violent lurch as the *Nerissa* settled further to port. Several of the passengers in the lifeboat screamed as they were thrown from side to side. The boat hung precariously in mid-air.

One of the hatches had not been secured properly, and the movement had sprung it open. As David watched in horror, two figures were flung outward from the protective shell and fell, tumbling over and over, into the black-blue waters below.

One of them was Deborah Corliss. And only David Spaulding knew the truth: she could not swim and was deathly afraid of the water.

10

Morgance had been watching for her chance. She knew she dare not wait much longer to make her escape. She still had the waterproof backpack strapped securely to her body, and it was stuffed to the brim with crisp new bank notes of all denominations. There was no way she was going to risk being searched by anyone, including any authorities who might be waiting for them when they landed.

All of the passengers had been informed that they were going to try to make their way to a nearby deserted island. Her problem was that she could not believe the authorities had not picked up on the location of the distressed ship. Her greatest fear was that either the FBI or some other international entity would intercept them on shore and search and question them to determine if any of them had had anything to do with the takeover of the ship.

She was still wearing the wetsuit under her loose clothing. She had already survived one jump into the sea, and she was a very strong swimmer.

When the ship buckled and the hatch nearest her seat popped open, she saw her chance and took it. It did not bother her that there was another woman sitting on the outside, next to the opening. She gave a mighty shove and followed the screaming victim through the hatch and into the sea below.

Once she had recovered from the immediate shock of entry, she struck out underwater with strong, regular strokes in a direction she thought was away from the activity of the lifeboats. Once she caught sight of the island, she would circumnavigate the area where the lifeboats were landing and try and get ashore in a less conspicuous spot. There she would hide and rest while the others were well occupied, then try and make her way to the other side of the island where, hopefully, she would find a few settlers and some way off to the mainland.

It was risky, but it was worth the

chance. If they caught her, they just might be able to link her to the murders in Illinois, not to mention what she had done on the ship. And she had no idea what had happened to Nevin. He was weak enough that he would probably rat her out if he was captured. All they would have to do would be to promise him immunity for his previous crimes. She had no doubt he would send her over without any qualms at all.

★ ★ ★

'No!' roared Dave when he realized it was Deb who had gone overboard. 'She can't swim!' he yelled to Richard, who was holding him back from climbing up over the now-slanting rail and jumping in as well.

'Maybe they can get her from down there,' Richard said. 'I don't think you'd ever find her now, jumping from up here. I can't — *won't* — let you do it, old man. Sorry.'

With Carl and Chip's help, Richard got David to one side and held on to him until he calmed down. 'I shouldn't have let her stay,' he moaned. 'I should have made her go on that first boat.'

'You can't change it now,' said Carl, 'as much as you want to. It's done. Richard's right — maybe they'll find her and pick her up from one of the other boats.'

'She wasn't the only one who went over,' said Richard. 'I thought I recognized the other woman. It was the one who interviewed her up on the Promenade Deck. Strange duck, I thought. I wonder if she was with anyone.' He looked around, but no one else seemed as distraught as David.

'I know who it was,' said a quiet voice behind them. The Canadian accent was unmistakable. The men all turned to stare at Nevin in surprise. He had been held back to go on the last boat under guard and had been watching all the activity with great interest.

'Who was it?' demanded Robbie. 'If you know who it was, it will help us when we go to file a report.'

'It was Morgance, of course,' Nevin said. His eyes were cold and he registered no emotion whatsoever. 'My partner; the one who killed the purser.'

'Do you think she jumped deliberately?' asked David. 'It looked as if she fell out behind Deb. You don't think . . . ' He stopped, stricken.

'That she pushed your Deborah out because she was in the way? It wouldn't surprise me,' Nevin said calmly. 'It wouldn't surprise me in the least. It's something she would be capable of doing, if someone stood in her way.'

★ ★ ★

As each lifeboat made landfall, it was met by a contingent of FBI and Homeland Security agents with weapons drawn. After a thorough questioning of Robbie's officers, who had been placed in charge of the rescue boats, they soon realized that whatever conspiracy had brought about this catastrophe, the situation was now well in hand.

As the shaken passengers made their way ashore, their names and identification were checked, and they were then led either to the emergency triage or a general waiting area that had been made as comfortable as possible on such short notice. Hot coffee and sandwiches had been prepared, and blankets were issued. Conrad Emerson's sheet-wrapped body had been brought ashore and was carried to a guarded tent near the triage, well out of the way of curious onlookers.

'Let's begin evacuating the ill and injured off the island immediately,' ordered Agent Kane. 'We need to get these people to safety as soon as possible. They've been through enough.'

His second-in-command trotted off to confer with the cadre of helicopter pilots who, under Kane's orders, had remained at the ready on a makeshift landing pad. They would begin shuttling the victims to several Coast Guard ships standing by near the island. He glanced back and with a thumbs-up gesture, began working his way through the crowd to the triage station.

'Now, I need to interview the captain.' Kane turned back to the others. 'I want to get a handle on just exactly what took place, and get his take on the major players.'

Agent Wright gestured to Robbie Jones, who was still overseeing the unloading of the prisoners off the last rescue boat. He gave a few instructions to his men before joining Kane.

The two men shook hands. 'Congratulations, Captain,' said Kane. 'Job well done. You've averted a major disaster here, under extremely difficult circumstances.'

'I can't take the credit, sir,' said Robbie. 'We were very lucky to have some very brave and talented men aboard who were willing to risk everything to save these people. They're the real heroes.'

'I'm glad to hear you say that,' said Kane. 'It's a welcome thing to know there are still good Samaritans left in the world. We see so much of the other kind that . . . well, let's just say it's like a breath of fresh air.'

'I know you'll need to debrief me,' Robbie went on. 'But I'd like to bring at least two others into the discussion as well. They know as much, or more, than I do about what happened. And they're the ones who were mainly responsible for putting the conspiracy to a stop.'

'I assume you're talking about the men from the Pittsburgh police force?' Kane scanned the beach, looking for them.

'Yes, sir, I am. The most resourceful of them is David Spaulding. He's really the man you should be interviewing. And you also need to speak with Dr. Richard Black Wolf, the well-known author and anthropologist. Between the two of them, those guys just didn't have a chance.'

'Fine, Captain.'

'Robbie, sir. Just call me Robbie. Everyone else does.'

The two men shook hands again and Kane gestured to Wright, who was standing nearby. 'Find David Spaulding and Richard Black Wolf. I'd like to include them in our discussions.'

Wright set off to pull the two friends away from their posts at the lifeboat landings, where they were still helping to direct people to assistance.

'Come on, guys,' he said when he found them. 'You're on. Boss-man wants to chat.'

David and Richard looked at each other. 'Uh, oh,' Richard said with a grin. 'I think we've blown our cover.'

★　★　★

David Spaulding smoothed his hair one more time, cleared his throat, and took his seat. This was the second such proceeding he had been summoned to attend in less than a year. And he was not looking forward to it, even though this time he was merely a witness and not a defendant, as he had been in his last appearance.

The investigative panel appointed by Homeland Security in conjunction with the International Maritime Organization was called to order. The participants, gathered in small groups about the humid Florida court room, had been discussing the situation in hushed tones, and now took their places.

The chairman cleared his throat. 'Good morning,' he began formally. 'I'm Paul Rogers, privileged to serve as chair of this panel, and I'd like to thank all of you for agreeing to appear here today. We plan to conduct an impartial, but thorough — and I emphasize *thorough* — hearing on the recent incidents resulting in the destruction of the Contessa Lines cruise ship *Nerissa* — incidents, I might add, which put the lives of all people aboard at risk.

'We have the bravery and quick-wittedness of Captain Jones, his officers and crew, and a small cadre of very selfless civilians who put their own lives at risk to save their fellow passengers.' He nodded in the direction of Robbie Jones who, in company with his senior officers, was seated at one of the front tables.

'I want also to commend Mr. David Spaulding, Dr. Richard Black Wolf, and their companions for not only uncovering the scheme to sink the *Nerissa*, but also for their clearheaded thinking and decisiveness in the face of an impending crisis, which prevented the culprits from profiting from their plot and brought them to justice.' He turned to David's group, seated in the first row just behind Jones.

'I understand also that Mr. Spaulding

suffered a significant personal loss during the struggle, and for that I wish to offer him the condolences of this commission and our deep regrets that he had to pay such a terrible price for his courage.'

David bowed his head, and Chip leaned over to pat his shoulder. After a moment he looked up again, his eyes bright with unshed tears.

'First, I would like to introduce Admiral Benjamin Thompson, who will act as overall counsel for Homeland Security and its arm, the United States Coast Guard, the Federal Bureau of Investigation and its Florida Field Office, the Legal Attaché's Office of Florida, and last but not least the Cruise Lines International Association, which has surrendered its jurisdiction in this matter to us.'

Admiral Thompson stood and acknowledged the participants. Once he was seated again, Rogers continued. 'Ralph Andrews of Andrews, Boyd and Sullivan, and Lloyd McCarthy of James and McCarthy, have agreed to act as attorneys for the defendants, namely: Kenway

Trumball, Amyas Stärke, Blake Bainbridge, Jr., *et al.*, including all known members of the organization known as the Foundation. It should be noted that Ms. Stärke is not present in the court today, and it is presumed that she may have lost her life when the ship capsized. All other unnamed participants will be dealt with in order, once decisions regarding the named defendants have been reached.'

He paused. 'There is another incident which took place on board the ship at about the same time, but we have determined there was no connection between the two events, and that particular case will be tried separately.'

He glanced at Nevin, seated under guard, to one side. The man had been brought in as a material witness to the Foundation takeover, but his own case would be addressed later on. Morgance still had not surfaced, and they were all saying she had probably died when she jumped off the lifeboat into the sea.

Nevin thought they might be wrong about that. And he was also beginning to worry that they might try to tie him to the Illinois murders. He squirmed in his seat. If only there was some way he could escape. He eyed the sidearm tucked into his guard's holster. Did he dare . . . ?

The chairman was droning on, going through the various technicalities of maritime law, the definition of what constituted piracy on the high seas, and the concept of claims to wreck salvage. Trumball's partner, the salvage-ship owner, had never made an attempt for the wreck, so there was some difficulty with holding and prosecuting him on conspiracy charges.

Just as Admiral Thompson stood to address the Cruise Line Association concerns, a loud popping noise from the side of the room brought them all to their feet.

'Look out!' called one of the guards. 'He's got a gun!'

Nevin, in his desperation, had made a terrible decision. Hoping to overpower his guard and grab the man's revolver, he instead tripped over his shackles and fell to the floor, the barrel of the gun in his hand — and pointed straight at his belly.

He sank in a quickly oozing pool of dark blood, which contrasted oddly with the bright orange jumpsuit all prisoners wear.

'Is he dead?' asked Rogers. After a quick inspection of the body and consultation among the guards, one stepped forward.

'No, sir. He was hit point blank in the gut, and I don't think he'll survive. But yes, he's still alive.' Sirens could be heard in the background, followed by footsteps pounding down the hallway. A team of paramedics, accompanied by more law-enforcement agents with guns drawn, made their way cautiously into the court room.

'It's all right,' Rogers called to them. 'He's unconscious and barely alive.' Turning to the assembly, he added, 'That's all. We're adjourned. You'll be notified when to reconvene. We may need a day or two to deal with all this.' He swept his hand toward the stretcher-borne Nevin being carried from the room.

David, Richard and the others filed out in silence. An aura of disbelief hung over them all. What more could happen?

11

It was exactly ten days before the panel met again, this time with decidedly fewer witnesses and spectators.

'Good morning,' intoned Paul Rogers. 'We are now in formal session, but a lot has gone on behind the scenes during the last week and a half.' He took a sip of water and cleared his throat. 'First, and most importantly perhaps, most of the surviving passengers of the *Nerissa* have now been processed, cleared of any wrong-doing, and allowed to return to their homes without further detainment. There is some talk of a class-action suit being pursued for their benefit against Contessa Lines, but it remains to be seen if there is any follow-through for that. I think most of the survivors are just grateful they were rescued, and many of them credit the ship's personnel and some of their fellow passengers for bringing that about.

'We've identified another small group of individuals who suffered mild to severe injuries or illnesses resulting from exposure and stress. Most have been treated and released to their own communities for further follow-up. Those with more severe issues have been hospitalized locally. They include the witness, Nevin Marmion. He is considered to be in grave condition, and his chances for a full recovery are minimal. An elderly woman is being treated for stress and exposure, and her condition is listed as guarded. The rest are all expected to recover completely. Yes?' He pointed to Admiral Thompson, who had raised his hand.

'As regards Mr. Marmion, has any disposition of his case been decided? Is there any chance we will be able to question him further? As you know, both the IMO and the Cruise Lines Association have concerns.'

'I'm going to get to all that in a moment, Admiral. Now, let's see . . . where was I?' He shuffled through the documents on his desk and conferred with the other panel members before continuing. 'I do want to address the issue of the deaths that we know occurred both during and after the attempted takeover of the ship. Because that is where, I believe, our difficulty lies. It seems, from what we have been able to determine, that there were not one but two separate and unrelated plots which took place within the same approximate time frame.'

There was a brief murmur amongst the onlookers, and several shook their heads in disbelief.

'What we know for certain is that the most dangerous conspiracy was concerned with the group known as the Foundation. The titular head of the cult was — *is* — a man named Kenway Trumball. But he was certainly aided and abetted by hard-core followers who were willing to risk their lives in an attempt to carry out this extremely dangerous and ill-thought-out scheme.

'The original plan, as hatched by Trumball and his closest associate, Amyas Stärke, was to convert as many of the other passengers as possible, to lead them in taking control of the ship, and to divert the *Nerissa* off its course to the deserted island of San Carlito. There they planned to scuttle the ship, leaving all unconverted passengers and the ship's crew to almost certain death trapped below decks. The Foundation members, in the meantime, would make their escape via the lifeboats to the deserted island.'

'But then what? What possible motive could they have for doing such a thing?' The speaker who had risen to his feet was a representative from CLIA, the cruise-line group.

'I'm getting to that. The second part of the scheme, and the real motive for sinking the ship, was the nearby *Scalawag*, a salvage ship owned and operated by Tommy Williams, who just happens to be the third partner in Kenway Trumball's plot.'

There was a stunned silence. The cruise ship rep sat back down and began jotting notes rapidly while Ralph Andrews bounded to his feet. 'I object to this whole proceeding,' began the counsel for Trumball and his accomplices. 'Much of this is hearsay. Surely my clients deserve an opportunity to defend themselves here.'

'This is *not* a formal court trial, Mr. Andrews, as you well know,' Rogers responded without anger. The man was simply doing his job. 'You are correct that many of these details need to be corroborated further, and there will be ample time for that at future trials — of which I am sure there will be many. But these proceedings are a preliminary attempt to get at the truth of what actually happened aboard that ship, and we will continue until we can resolve some of these issues in a fair and impartial manner. Please be seated and let me continue my narration. It is, in my opinion, imperative that we reach some sort of consensus about what occurred before we can even begin to discuss trials and court procedures.'

'Yes, sir,' replied Andrews. 'But I must insist on registering my concern that this proceeding is being conducted in a highly irregular manner.'

'Your concerns are duly noted,' acknowledged Rogers, nodding at the recording clerk busy compiling the transcript.

'Now, where were we? Yes. Tommy Williams, a licensed salvage-ship operator, would be standing by. As soon as the ship was sunk, he would wait until Kenway and his followers were safely on the island. Then he would report the 'accident' to the Coast Guard — and simultaneously file a claim for salvage.'

'But what about the rights of the cruise line?' asked Thompson, anticipating his clients' concerns.

'Well, that's a gray area, isn't it?' Rogers noted. 'It all depends, really, on who gets there first. If he's right there at the spot he can make a legitimate request to be allowed to salvage what he can from the remains of the ship. The cruise line can, of course, object to that and put in their own claims. I've seen these cases go for years in the courts before a decision can be made.

'What I suspect, without confirmation from Trumball or Williams, is that an offer would be made to 'settle' with the cruise line. They would relinquish their claims in return for some sort of settlement or ransom from Contessa. It might, or might not, be worth the company's effort to raise the ship. Either way, Williams, and through him Trumball, stood to make a sizeable amount of money out of this venture. Certainly enough to finance the Foundation's activities for quite a while.'

Rogers then called for a break before continuing with the next portion of his exposition.

David Spaulding and Richard Black Wolf gulped down bitter black coffee from the vending machine in the hallway just outside the courtroom.

'What I really don't get,' David said, 'is why Kenway and his thugs thought they wouldn't be investigated if they were rescued off the island. Didn't they realize they would have to go through just what we're doing today?'

'I doubt they thought it through that far.' Richard tossed his empty cup into the trash. 'I think they believed they would be 'rescued' and treated like survivors of an accident. We know, of course, that the authorities would have delved a bit deeper into their IDs and discovered all the connections — but I think they did expect to get away with it. Even if we hadn't managed to put a stop to their plot, I think they would have been under suspicion and brought to trial anyway. At least we managed to save a few lives.'

He had forgotten for a moment about David's loss. 'Sorry,' he said.

'It's all right. I have to start dealing with it. Look, they're getting ready to start up again. Let's go.'

★　★　★

'And now we come to what is the most puzzling, and troublesome, part of our investigation.' Paul Rogers paused and looked down at his notes. 'Unbeknownst to Kenway Trumball and his associates, and certainly unknown to Captain Jones and his crew, two other nefarious individuals managed to inveigle their way aboard.

'A few nights before the *Nerissa* was scheduled to depart from her berth at

Port Everglades, two vicious murders were committed in Barrington Hills, Illinois, a small upscale suburb near Chicago. An elderly couple, Norman and Mildred O'Conner, were lured to sign up for a cruise as recipients of a sweepstakes prize. The prize was awarded to them as part of a scheme initiated, as we have been able to discover, by members of the Russian Mafia — in other words, international mobsters.'

There was a buzz of consternation throughout the room, which continued until Roger gently gaveled for silence. 'The perpetrators of the Illinois crime were a couple of French-Canadian nationals who travelled frequently in and out of the United States, sometimes with valid ID, sometimes not. They were small-time grifters and petty criminals — until meeting up with the Russians.

'Then a plot was hatched. The Russians, through their connections, would 'fix' the outcome of the sweepstakes. The elderly couple was chosen at random, but they had to be in a relatively secluded area, and without children or relatives who would be likely to check on them right away. Once the killing took place, the killers would assume their identities. The pair, donning elaborate disguises, became 'Mr. and Mrs. O'Conner,' and under those names they boarded the *Nerissa* and sailed on her.

'Once they were well out to sea, their assignment was to compromise the ship's satellite array in the communications area and re-program it with coordinates to be relayed to a designated Russian satellite in orbit around the earth.

'We have yet to determine the ultimate goal of the mobsters, since our only witness as to their possible motives is one of the culprits, Nevin Marmion, who, as you all know, is in grave condition and not expected to survive. We suspect, however, that it may be part of some kind of international plot to hack into banks and credit card accounts all over the world.'

There was a gasp from the audience. Dave and Richard looked at each other and grimaced. So *that* was what it was all about.

'Makes sense,' Richard whispered. 'A scheme like that could be worth billions, ultimately.'

'In any case, the female partner, a woman known variously as Morgance Searlait or, on occasion, 'Margeaux Surlotte,' is . . . ' He paused for effect. 'She's either dead at the bottom of the sea, or she managed to escape during the offloading of the passengers. If so, we have no idea where she is or what name she might be traveling under.

'What we *do* know is that she is a vicious and manipulative killer. What's more, she is a master disguise artist. She could be anywhere in the world at this moment, posing as someone completely different, both in name and appearance. In other words, we have no idea where she is.'

★　★　★

The rest of the proceeding went quickly and smoothly. There were only a few more issues to settle.

Kenway Trumball and his closest

associates, including his mini-army of thugs, would be held for trial on criminal charges. It was hoped that with the mounds of evidence and testimony lodged against them, they would be swiftly brought to justice and put under lock and key for a very long time.

The lesser members of the cult, including those like Doreen, who had been taken in during the cruise, would be dealt with much less harshly. It was hoped that most of them could be released under their own recognizance, with stipulations of rehabilitative treatment in their own towns coupled with community service as recompense. Likely, most would be cooperative.

Blake Bainbridge, Jr., with his father's support, and with positive testimony provided by Captain Jones, David Spaulding and Richard Black Wolf, was completely cooperative in his role as a material witness against the Foundation. He was remanded into his father's custody and would undergo both in- and out-patient treatment therapies for his physical, mental and psychological disorders.

Blake Bainbridge, Sr. donated a significant sum to the International Survivors' Reparation Fund, and paid the Contessa Lines organization a substantial amount as well for the part his son had played in the takeover plot.

Nevin Marmion never recovered consciousness. He remained intubated and medically sedated throughout the preliminary investigation and hearing, in the hope he might eventually be able to provide more insight into his partner's possible whereabouts. At the end of the proceedings, however, he was declared brain-dead and removed from life support. There were few attendees, and no tears were shed, at his brief service in Fort Lauderdale's Pauper's Field.

'At least we were able to question him pretty thoroughly before he attempted to escape,' David commented to Richard as they stood in the background while the little man's body was lowered into the ground.

The whereabouts of the woman known as Morgance Searlait remained a mystery. Her last known physical description, and the names she had been known to use, remained on file as an open case within the bowels of the FBI and were broadcast worldwide through Interpol and other international policing organizations. It was assumed that she was lying low, perhaps on one of the Caribbean's pristine white beaches, until enough time passed when she could safely retrieve her ill-gotten goods from the Swiss bank account Nevin had mentioned before his death.

The bodies of Amyas Stärke and Kostya Varvarinski were both recovered when the sunken *Nerissa* was raised from its ocean grave. Kenway's request to attend Amyas's burial was denied, and both she and Kostya were laid to rest with no fanfare in the same dismal cemetery as Nevin. Again, no tears were shed for these two.

David Spaulding returned to Pittsburgh with Carl and Chip and their wives. The funeral honoring Conrad Emerson was well-attended by his fellow police officers, both past and present, and his body was laid to rest near his parents in their family plot.

Deborah's body was never recovered

but, given her lack of swimming ability, David knew she could not have survived that plunge into the ocean's icy depths for long. He and their friends held an intimate memorial for her, and a fund to assist deserving young nursing students was established in her name at the hospital where she had spent so much time in recent years.

Richard Black Wolf took a sabbatical from his tours and appearances and settled down to write a book about his experiences aboard the *Nerissa*. His publishers and agent were ecstatic. With all the publicity surrounding the takeover and scuttling of the ship, they were sure it would make a fortune for them, and the advance was significant. After sending a substantial portion to his family, as he always did, he donated the rest of it to the Survivors Reparations Fund, in spite of Martin Abbott's dismay.

'What are you doing, man?' Marty said, shaking his head. 'We *all* coulda retired on that!'

'In spite of everything you've been told and everything you believe,' Richard said with a grin, 'money is *not* the be-all and end-all of existence. I'm perfectly content. And *you* need to relax. Trust me. There'll be a lot more where that came from, you can bet on it.'

A few days after Conrad Emerson was laid to rest, David, Carl and Chip were honored in a highly publicized ceremony at City Hall in downtown Pittsburgh. The mayor, in a moving presentation, noted that 'these three men, through their courage, initiative and concern for others, represented their city in the most honorable manner possible' and that 'without their willingness to 'protect and serve,' many of their fellow passengers would not have survived.' Shiny medals of honor were pinned to their uniformed chests, and the rest of the day was spent in general celebration.

'Well, guys,' said Carl, raising his glass as they sat around a big table in their favorite watering hole, 'I guess this is about as good as it gets. Here's lookin' at you.' He downed his drink in one gulp and signaled for another round.

'Here's to Dave,' added Chip. 'Man,

you really came through on this one. I take back everything I ever said about that other . . . Well, let's just say I stand corrected.' He, too, drained his glass.

David smiled. This was a bittersweet moment for him. He had proved himself, yes. But in the midst of the celebration, all he could think of right now was what he had lost. Connie, his mentor, was one thing. The old man *had* been a surrogate father to him. Flawed, yes, he now realized, but always caring and supportive. He would miss that connection.

Most of all, he grieved for Deborah. He understood the truth now of the old maxim, 'You never appreciate what you have until you lose it.' He had taken her for granted. And he regretted that now. But he was philosophical enough to accept that he could not change what had happened. He only hoped that she had died knowing just how much she meant to him.

'I've got an announcement to make,' he said finally, taking a sip of his own drink. 'As of tomorrow, I am no longer working for the Pittsburgh Police Department.' He let a moment pass for that to sink in as the others stared at him in concern.

'What . . . ?' began Carl.

'No, hear me out,' Dave continued. 'This is good news for me. Following all the hearings, I got a phone call from that FBI guy, Wright Weatherby. Seems they've been discussing all that's happened in great detail.'

'But what's that got to do with — ' Chip interrupted.

'I'm getting to that. I guess you guys know that one of my greatest ambitions was to one day make detective. I think I've always wanted to be involved with the forensic side of things; just never had the gumption or ambition to go for it. To make a long story short, I've been offered an opportunity to join the FBI as an intern of sorts.'

The two cops gaped at their friend in amazement. 'But — ' Carl started.

'And what's more, I've accepted. I start training in their behavioral sciences program next week. I'm really excited about this, and I hope you guys will wish me luck.'

'That's great, Dave!' said Chip firmly, offering his hand over the table. 'I'm really proud of you. If anyone deserves this break, it's you.'

'Same thing here, fella,' added Carl, pounding Dave on the shoulder. 'Just don't forget us old cops back here, that's all. We'll be pullin' for ya!'

'I won't forget any of you, I promise. I'll have to move on base down at Quantico temporarily, but who knows? I could be assigned back to this area eventually. In any case, I'll get breaks. We can all meet on a regular basis.'

'Yeah,' said Chip. 'Who knows? We might even decide to take a cruise together someday!'

Other titles in the
Linford Mystery Library:

HOLLYWOOD HEAT

Arlette Lees

1950s Los Angeles: When six-year-old Daisy Adler vanishes from her upscale Hollywood Hills home, Detective Rusty Hallinan enters a case with more dangerous twists and turns than Mulholland Drive. Hallinan's life hits a bump or two of its own when he's dumped by his wife and falls for an enchanting young murder suspect half his age. But what's the connection between her murdered husband and a dying bar-room stripper? How does Hallinan's informant, exotic and endangered female impersonator Tyrisse Covington, fit into the puzzle? And where has little Daisy gone?

THE WITCHES' MOON

Gerald Verner

Mr. Dench left his house on a wet September night to post a letter at a nearby pillar-box — and disappeared. A fortnight later his dead body was found in a tunnel a few miles away. He had been brutally murdered. Called in to investigate, Superintendent Robert Budd soon realizes that Dench hadn't planned to disappear. But it's not until he finds the secret of the fireman's helmet, the poetic pickpocket, and the Witches' Moon that he discovers why Mr. Dench — and several other people — have been murdered . . .